Charlie glanced at Lewis. He was looking right at her.

He was so close. Close enough to touch, to kiss. And she'd seen the old Lewis a few moments ago, laughing and playing, uninhibited by disappointment or sadness. She had a sudden ache to run her fingers across his jaw. To press her mouth against his.

Whoa. Really? But then, the physical side of their relationship had never been the problem. Their desire for each other had been insatiable.

Did he feel the same need?

Dear Reader,

I do love a reunion story. What's better than to watch the love and attraction our couple originally had grow and develop...but not without some stumbling blocks along the way! (Oh, the evil mind of a romance writer!)

When Lewis and Charlotte's marriage tragically broke up five years ago, neither of them could see a way through the sadness of it all or ever imagine being in another relationship again. But when an accident brings them together, they are forced to confront all the reasons for their breakup and are shocked to find themselves unable to deny their sizzling attraction.

But are the embers of their love enough for them to try again? Well, that depends on trust, and when one person has already walked away once, what are the chances they might do it again? Oh, poor Charlie and Lewis. I loved writing their Auckland-set story and seeing them fight hard against their attraction and then learn to fight for themselves and each other.

I hope you enjoy *Winning Back His Runaway Wife*. Thank you for taking a chance on one of my books. Catch up with my news at www.louisageorge.com.

Happy reading!

Louisa xxx

WINNING BACK HIS RUNAWAY WIFE

LOUISA GEORGE

MEDICAL ROMANCE

Harlequin® MEDICAL ROMANCE

ISBN-13: 978-1-335-59546-1

Winning Back His Runaway Wife

Copyright © 2024 by Louisa George

Harlequin Enterprises ULC
22 Adelaide St. West, 41st Floor
Toronto, Ontario M5H 4E3, Canada
www.Harlequin.com

Printed in U.S.A.

Recycling programs for this product may not exist in your area.

Award-winning author **Louisa George** has been an avid reader her whole life. In between chapters, she's managed to train as a nurse, marry her doctor hero and have two sons. Now she writes chapters of her own in the medical romance, contemporary romance and women's fiction genres. Louisa's books have variously been nominated for the coveted RITA® Award and the New Zealand Koru Award and have been translated into twelve languages. She lives in Auckland, New Zealand.

Books by Louisa George

Harlequin Medical Romance

A Sydney Central Reunion

Ivy's Fling with the Surgeon

Rawhiti Island Medics

Resisting the Single Dad Next Door

Royal Christmas at Seattle General

The Princess's Christmas Baby

A Puppy and a Christmas Proposal
Nurse's One-Night Baby Surprise
ER Doc to Mistletoe Bride
Cornish Reunion with the Heart Doctor
Reunited by the Nurse's Secret

Visit the Author Profile page
at Harlequin.com for more titles.

To Flo Nicoll, the best editor any writer could ask for. Thank you for taking a chance on me and for encouraging and supporting my writing dreams. And to the Harlequin Medical Romance team, thank you so much for bringing me into your family and making my writing dreams come true!

**Praise for
Louisa George**

"A single dad, an unexpected pregnancy, secret crush, friends to lovers, Louisa George combines so many of my favourite tropes in her latest outing to Oakdale... This series is right up there with Sarah Morgan's medical romances...and it's no secret how much I love those."
—*Goodreads* on *Nurse's One-Night Baby Surprise*

CHAPTER ONE

FIVE YEARS AGO Charlotte Rose would have cherished this moment.

This...exact...moment: clipping the most adorable, smiling baby into her car seat after a night of nine hours' sleep—nine whole hours! And she was only six months old. Baby Stella was a veritable miracle of cuteness overload. Climbing into the driver's seat and heading across the city she loved to a job she adored: part-time emergency doctor at busy Auckland Central hospital. And enjoying the whole Auckland summer vibe of sunshine, sparkling waterfront views and, today, surprisingly little traffic.

Five years ago, Charlotte would have thought this scenario would make her life utterly complete: a baby; the perfect job with hours to suit; being back in her beloved hometown. But here she was, wishing everything could be different.

From the back seat baby Stella made a little hiccupping noise. Charlotte's heart jolted, knowing that specific sound was a precursor to... Oh, yes: here it came, loud and heart-wrenching, not just a cry but a full-on bawl.

Smiling, Charlotte glanced in her mirror and cooed, 'Stella, Stella, sweetie. Please don't cry. Hush. Hush.'

The baby had been fed, nappy-changed and had a toy to play with for the short drive. Maybe she'd dropped it. Ah, well, it would have to wait.

Charlotte switched the talkback radio station to something with upbeat music, hoping that would soothe her precious cargo. Sure enough, Stella blinked, mouth open. A pause….? A reprieve…? Yes…? Yes…?

Then she inhaled deeply and started with that heart-breaking sound again.

No.

'Stella, darling. Please don't cry. It's all going to be okay.'

Please let it all be okay.

Charlotte sighed, wondering whether she should pull over, find the dropped toy and give Stella a quick cuddle because, yes, she was a softie who would rather cradle a baby than let it cry. And why not? Babies didn't understand timetables and deadlines. Didn't know about having to go to work. One quick smooch wouldn't hurt. Maybe Stella needed a drink or a snack.

She spied a good parking spot across the other side of the traffic lights. She cooed some more as they sat idling at the front of the car line, waiting at the intersection until the lights turned green. Then she headed across…

A shadow whooshed across her line of vision. Her neck and upper body jerked as she felt an impact, as if she were a rag doll being shaken. Then her car was shunted from the side, across the road, out of control.

What the hell?

Panic made her hands shake, made her limbs weak and her heart race. She managed to turn her head to work out what the hell was going on. The front of a huge truck was glued to her door. There was a screech of tires. The stench of burning rubber. The crunch of metal on concrete. A looming lamp post.

And a very quiet baby.

CHAPTER TWO

'MATE, MIA'S FRIENDS *loved* you. She said to tell you that any time you fancy coming over again for a break we can organise a double date…'

'Thanks, but no.' Lewis Parry laughed but jumped in to shut his colleague up. Being on holiday for two weeks with Brin and his family on Rāwhiti Island had been amazing. They'd gone fishing, swimming and diving. They'd eaten what they'd caught from the ocean and drunk the local craft beer. 'I had a great holiday and I've come back to work feeling refreshed and relaxed. In my experience, a relationship would put a swift end to that kind of vibe.'

'Just saying…' Brin put up his hands. 'I thought the same, but find the right woman and it all clicks into place.'

Been there. Done that. And it all fell apart.

'I'm thinking you got lucky.' Lewis finished up his electronic notes from their last call out and slipped the tablet into the glove box. Sometimes he wished he worked in wide open spaces rather than the confines of an ambulance with a newly ordained and far too enthusiastic matchmaker as sidekick.

'You have to make your own luck, mate.' Brin grinned. 'Hey, maybe you'll make some luck at the fundraiser on Saturday night. Lots of hospital staff will be there...' He winked and nudged Lewis's arm.

Great. Brin's happily settled so he thinks we all have to be.

The radio crackled.

'Code Red. R Four. MVA. Female driver. Baby passenger. Ponsonby Road and Picton Street intersection.'

Lewis was immediately grateful for the spotlight shifting from his woeful love life to their jobs.

'Ten-two. Unit Four responding. Over,' he radioed back to control. Then he turned to Brin. 'A baby? Damn. Let's get a move on.'

As they approached the accident scene, it was obvious that a truck had ploughed into the side of an old blue sedan which had then been shunted into a lamp post. The car's rear driver's side door had been totalled and the driver's door buckled and dented enough to impede opening. The passenger-side doors rear and front were dented but openable. He assessed the area for safety as he jumped from the van: no evidence of spilt petrol or oil.

The truck driver was sitting on the side of the road, head in hands.

Lewis called out, 'You okay? Do you need help?'

Face pale and wan, the man shook his head. 'Help the others. I'm… I'm okay. My brakes… I kept pressing on them but they didn't…'

'Thanks, man. We'll come back to you and check you over.' The man was walking and talking: he could wait. Lewis turned to Brin. 'I'll check the driver, you check the baby.'

'On it.' Brin nodded and peeled off to the far side of the car.

The driver's window was smashed and Lewis had a partial view of the person in the driving seat as he tried to tug open the distorted door. She had her head turned away, looking into the back seat. Her shoulders were shaking, and she was saying something he couldn't quite hear. Her hair—a beautiful shade of russet red—was tied into a low ponytail.

Red…

Charlie?

A long-forgotten ache slammed into his gut, mingling with memories he'd tried to keep at bay for five years. Memories that flashed through his mind: red hair entwined with flowers and a gossamer veil; red hair splayed on a pillow as they'd made love. A tight ponytail, shoulders shuddering as she'd walked away, suitcase in hand—the last image of her as she'd left him.

No, it couldn't be Charlie. He shook himself. She lived in London. But funny-weird how, even though she lived on the opposite side of the world, he sometimes thought he saw her at the beach, in a crowded street or in a shopping mall.

It was never her.

Focus, man.

Her screams were becoming clearer now. 'The baby! Is the baby okay? *Please.* Please get the baby.'

Definitely not Charlie. There were no babies in her life; there couldn't be. But as she turned to look at him, her blue eyes red-rimmed and imploring, cheeks streaked with running mascara, his gut folded in on itself. It felt as if the world had stopped turning. It was her, with her mesmerising eyes and perfect mouth.

His wife.

Ex-wife.

'Charlie?'

'Lewis?' Her chest caved forward then, and her face crumpled. 'Oh, my God, Lewis, thank God it's you. You've got to help me. Please, get the baby. She's too quiet.'

Damn. Was it her baby? He pushed the spike of hurt away. 'It's okay, Charlie. My colleague's opening the door now. He'll check your baby. What's her name?'

'St... Stella,' Charlie stuttered through gulps of air. 'Is she okay? Please make sure she's okay.'

'It's okay, it's okay, I can hear her fussing,' He lowered his voice and crouched to talk to her. Charlie was his patient now. Their past had nothing to do with this. He needed to be the paramedic, despite his shaking hands. *Damn.* She'd always had this effect on him: taking his breath away, tipping his world sideways. 'She doesn't look hurt at all. The car seat kept her safe. My colleague Brin will look after Stella. I'm here for you. Tell me, where do *you* hurt?'

The front airbag hadn't activated. It was an old car, and probably didn't even have side bags.

'I don't know.' She looked down at her trembling hands and his eyes followed: no wedding ring. There was no ring at all where her platinum bands used to be. 'I think… I'm okay. My chest hurts a little. And my shoulder…it's not bad. Probably from the seatbelt.'

'I bet. You want me to take a look?'

She edged sideways away from him and for a moment he thought she was recoiling at his suggestion, but in fact she was making room in the tight space. 'I think it's just bruised. Yes, look—check.'

Her gaze caught his and for a moment his need to look after her almost overwhelmed him, even after all these years apart. Even after she'd walked away.

He drew his gaze from hers. Just looking at her made his heart sore. He couldn't bear to see her hurting too, and he reached in and moved the soft fabric of her blouse away from her shoulder. Her familiar perfume of rose and sweet citrus hung in the air, spinning him back in time. 'Ouch. Yes, it's red raw. You're going to have a nasty bruise there. Do your ribs hurt?' He quickly moved his hand away and closed down more memories that assaulted his brain.

She blinked up at him and something flickered across her eyes: gratitude? He wasn't sure. She gave him a shoddy attempt at a smile. 'Only if I move.'

'So, stay still. What about your feet? Legs?' He could see bent metal close to her knees but not around her feet. It was a miracle she hadn't been badly hurt.

'They're okay, not hurt. I'm just wedged in by the door. Oh, Lewis, I need to get to work. But I need… I can't leave Stella. I can't take her to nursery. Not now after this.'

Work? She lived here now?

'Oh, no, you don't.' He peered into the car and tried to get a better view of her body so he could assess for any more injuries. 'We need to get you out of this vehicle and checked out at the hospital. You're in shock. You could be hurt and not even realise—whiplash, for example.'

'Hey.' Brin came round to this side of the car, a baby cradled in his arms. 'Someone needs their mama.'

Charlie's face filled with love and panic. 'Is she…?'

Brin grinned. 'She seems fine, love. A little bewildered by all the drama, but absolutely fine. I'll give her a proper check in a minute, but thought you'd want to see her first.'

'Thank God.' Relief flooded Charlie's face as she reached through the cracked window and stroked little Stella's head. 'I'm sorry, baby. I love you. You're okay. You're okay.'

The baby gurgled and giggled, her arms stretched out to be held by her mother. But Charlie smiled through her tears and shook her head. Lewis recognised the brave face she'd spent a good eighteen months out of their four-year marriage trying to put on as she cooed, 'Hey, hey, baby. I'm a bit stuck. I'll hold you when I can get out of here.'

Lewis's gut hollowed out.

Charlie and a baby: all they'd ever wanted.

But how? It didn't matter, right? She'd got the baby she'd so desperately wanted…just with another guy.

He tugged again at the door and breathed out in relief at the sound of a siren. 'Sounds like help is on its way. We'll get you out in no time.'

'The car is wrecked.' She shook her head.

'Thank God it was just the car, right?'

She put her head on the steering wheel. 'Ugh. Lucy's going to kill me.'

'It's Lucy's car?'

'Yes. I haven't had time to find one for me yet.' She slowly sat up and rubbed her shoulder. 'And I don't even know what happened. How the hell am I going to explain this?'

So she hadn't been back long enough to buy herself a car. Why was she back? And why did he care? Why did it matter? They were ancient history. She'd been so unhappy back then she'd fled to the other side of the world without him. What mattered now was that she and her baby were safe and unhurt.

'Truck driver said his brakes failed.'

'Oh. I guess it could have been much worse.' She closed her eyes and swallowed, as if imaging what worse would look like.

'Do you want me to call her—Lucy? Your parents? Call…someone else?' She'd moved on, right? Was Stella's father still in the picture?

'No!' Her eyes flashed pure panic for a brief moment, then she relaxed. 'No, it's fine. I'll call Lucy when I'm done at the hospital.'

'Okay…' He thought about asking her more about some significant other she might need to call, but thought better of it. It wasn't his business.

But she was still looking at him. 'Look, Lewis, I need to explain…'

'Like I said, the truck driver seems to be taking responsibility.' He got the feeling she wasn't referring to the accident, but he didn't want to get into anything deeper here. She had a family now; she'd moved on. Just as he had...*kind of.* Sure, he'd thought he had, but the ache at seeing her again had blindsided him. 'Honestly. We just need to get you safe. The firies are almost here; I can hear the sirens. They'll lever the door open, then we can take you and your baby to Central.'

She put her hand to her head. 'Ugh. A patient at my own workplace. That sucks.'

'You're working there?'

'Yes. I came back a few weeks ago. It's a long—'

'Hey, Lewis. Missy's getting a bit antsy.' Brin handed him the baby who was now wriggling and fretting—not quite crying but it was a definite overture before the big crescendo. 'Can you have a go at soothing her? She might like your face better than mine.'

'Damn right she will,' Lewis quipped with a smile that he didn't feel as he took baby Stella into his arms. She was a good weight, about six months old, maybe seven. Same shock of red hair as her mother. She was healthy; cute as a damned button.

He cleared his throat as it had become surprisingly raw all of a sudden. 'Um...hey, you. Look who's here. She's right here. And she wants to give you a cuddle, but she's stuck in the car. So you're stuck with me.'

Little Stella gazed up at him and tapped his nose with her little fist. She had huge navy eyes which were swimming with tears. Lewis's heart contracted. *No.* He did not want to feel anything. Not the hurt he'd felt at Charlotte leaving. Not the tug towards her that was as natural as breathing. Not the softening, or the care. He did not want those things again—ever.

This was not Charlie's and his baby, but his chest hurt, his throat burning as he held her. Panicked, he turned to hand her back to Brin, but he was over checking on the truck driver.

So, there he was, holding his ex-wife's much-wanted baby with feet feeling like clay and his chest like a vice around his heart. A weird and unexpected start to a Monday morning.

''Scuse me, mate.' A fire fighter in full yellow uniform was standing behind him holding the metal 'jaws of life' hydraulic rescue tool. 'Give us some room, yeah?'

'Sure.' Lewis swallowed back all the emotion rattling through him and rocked the baby up and down, pulling faces at her to try make her laugh. Maybe she was scared at seeing her mummy stuck in the car. Maybe this kind of thing traumatised a kid. Or maybe she was too young for it to make a difference.

He only knew of his own experiences—that what adults did and said, or neglected to do and neglected to say, had a lasting effect. So he turned away from the car and showed Stella the seagull sitting on top of the damaged lamp post, the flowers on the grass verge and an aeroplane high in the sky.

'You're a natural.'

What?

He whirled round to see Charlotte standing in front of him. Her face was damp from tears, her expression soul-deep sad and her cheeks now red with a blush. 'Um… I said, you're a natural. With the baby, I mean.'

He didn't know what to say; he did not want to go over old history. Talking about the past didn't change what had happened. Better to hold his guard and keep schtum.

And…there was the root of all their problems. He'd spent the last five years mentally unravelling their unravelling. Perhaps…*maybe*…he could have said more back then instead of keeping it all balled up inside him instead of trying to bolster her up to his own detriment and feeding her… not lies, exactly, but little wishes he'd wanted to be true. He should have ditched the stoicism and just been outright, totally, unequivocally honest.

But he'd thought he was doing the right thing. He'd done what he'd learnt to do: biting back his own truths, because no one wanted to hear your problems. No one wanted to hear how you feel.

She held out her hands for her baby, which he gave her gladly. Her eyes roamed her daughter's face, then her body, as if checking for signs of injury. 'There you are. You're okay, you're just perfect.' Then she smooched the little girl's face with kisses. When she seemed satisfied all was okay, she turned back to Lewis. 'Brin says we have to go to hospital, and I think I should get Stella checked out. I mean, I'm okay, but I want to be sure about her.'

'Of course. Very wise. Get your neck and shoulder checked too.'

'Are you…in the back of the ambulance? Will you be there…with us?' Worry nipped at her features.

He shook his head. 'I'm driver today.'

Her eyebrows rose. 'Oh.'

He couldn't identify the emotion behind that word. Relief that they wouldn't be in an enclosed space together or disappointment? Why did he hope it was the latter? Oh, poor, pathetic heart.

She left you, mate. Reel it in.

Brin, oblivious to *everything*, laughed and opened the back doors of the ambulance. 'He thinks I'm too Perez to be a paramedic.'

She frowned as she climbed into the back of the van. 'Perez?'

'He's a Formula One racing-car driver.' Lewis found a smile. 'Trust me, it's safer this way.'

Trust me.

Another knife to his heart.

Trust me to listen, to support. To grow with you. To be flexible. To change as we change.

Yet he'd done none of those things, although

he'd tried damned hard. It just hadn't been enough, apparently.

It was all too late now anyway.

He turned and walked to the front of his van, readying himself to take her to the hospital, her place of work. The place he visited on a very regular basis. The place where he was going to see her daily, probably more than that, handing over patients, sharing the lunchroom space, the café and the corridors.

Up until today he hadn't realised how easier his life had been, knowing she was at the other side of the world and that he wouldn't bump into her here in Auckland. Or how much effect she would still have on him even after five years apart.

But Charlotte Rose was back and she was going to haunt his working days now, as well as his nights.

CHAPTER THREE

TELLING LUCY ABOUT the accident was one of the worst things Charlie had ever done, even though they were both just fine—apart from Charlie's chest and shoulder bruising. But she'd broken the news gently and reassured her sister that they were both okay.

Lucy shrugged the blankets off her knee and slowly sat up from her prone position on the couch, taking Stella in her arms. 'Poor baby. A car crash? What an adventure.'

'An adventure? I wish I had your slant on things. I'm supposed to be here to help you, not cause even more stress.' But, when she looked at her sister, Charlie saw the pain she was hiding. The worry lines that made her look older than her thirty-eight years: the dark rings under her eyes; the slack skin from her weight loss—a direct result of the disease inside her—and the medication that was poisoning her and curing her in equal measure.

Lucy sighed. 'You're being a massive help. You know I couldn't have gone through this on my own. I'm so grateful you came back. Hell, you gave up your whole London life for me and Stella. Come sit down, Charlie. You look terrible, so pale and shocked. I'll get the kettle on.'

'No, I'm fine, really. Just a bit bruised and heart sore. I'd hate anything to happen to Stella, especially if it was on my watch. Sit.' She mock-glared at her sister, who was supposed to be resting. 'You stay here, and I'll get the kettle on. Maybe we can go sit outside in the sun for a while.'

'Oh, yes please. And let's have the ginger biscuits. I'm starving.'

'That's great. The nausea has settled, then?'

'I'm trying to ignore it.' Lucy shook her head and smiled wanly. 'I need to keep my strength up for this little one.'

'That's why I'm here to help.' Charlie sat down next to her sister.

Lucy's eyes glistened with tears, showing a rare chink in her 'I'll be fine' armour. 'I love you. Thank you.'

'I love you too.' Charlie circled her arms round her older sister and hugged her gently, so glad she'd come back to help her.

She'd been away too long, licking her own wounds after her infertility diagnosis and failed marriage, and had only barely acknowledged her family's attempts to connect. But getting that call from a terrified Lucy had been the shake-up Charlie had needed. Lucy hadn't wanted to spoil their parents' overseas charity-work trip of a lifetime, as they'd no doubt have rushed back to help out, so the first person she'd called was her sister. Charlie had jumped at the chance to walk this cancer journey with her.

And she was not going to lambast Lucy's ex-boyfriend for not stepping up to help look after his child. It was none of her business, and his loss. But the way Lucy was handling things now was impressive.

'I don't understand how you can be so upbeat when you must be knackered after the chemo.' One round down, six more to go…. maybe…hopefully…and a long road to recovery.

'Hey, I feel like crap, yes. But I choose to be positive. Look, I still have my hair. And my sense of humour.' Lucy pulled a funny face, although they both knew that the hair would be gone soon. Charlie just hoped Lucy could maintain her sunny outlook through the gruelling treatment. Lucy sighed and snuggled her daughter. 'It could all have been worse.'

'That's what I said to Lewis—'

'Oh my God, you saw Lewis?' Lucy's eyes widened. 'You kept that quiet.'

'I thought it was more important that I told you about the accident than the attending paramedic.'

'But, wow, imagine that. You have an accident and the paramedic is your ex-husband. Thank God you parted agreeably.'

'Yeah. Imagine.' She hadn't gone into a lot of

detail with her family about the reasons for her marriage break-up, although they knew it had been to do with her infertility.

But she hadn't been aware her sister thought it had been an agreeable split. In truth, they'd barely been speaking. Communication had dwindled over months until they'd been more like distant flatmates than married partners. But there hadn't been any raging arguments or outward bitterness, just sadness that they hadn't been able to make it as a couple. Sadness that Charlie had taken a long time to shake off.

In truth, she hadn't known what to say about seeing Lewis. Their meeting was inevitable, given where she now worked, and she'd thought she'd prepared herself for seeing him in the flesh. But nothing could have equipped her for the onslaught of emotions—happiness and bone-deep sadness—that had accompanied the panic of being in an MVA and the relief at having him, of all people, help her.

'How did it go? What was he like?'

Still gorgeous.

Through the haze of panic, fear and, yes, some pain, she hadn't been immune to his beautiful, soulful brown eyes and dazzling smile. He'd always taken her breath away with that smile. And the way he'd gently examined her shoulder, the look in his eyes filled with emotion, had made her heart squeeze. She remembered the way he used

to look at her, with such affection and love, then…
disappointment. Although he'd never admit it.

'I was just glad he was there. He's very good at
his job and made me feel a lot better—very professional. He checked Stella over. Distracted her
from anything that might have scared her.'

'Did you talk? You know, about what happened?'

'We didn't talk about anything, Luce. I was his
patient, then I was taken to hospital and he left to
go to his next call-out.'

Lucy frowned. 'Not even a brief conversation?'

'About what? How? He was busy and working.
You'd never have known we even knew each other,
never mind been married.'

'Still tight-lipped about his feelings, then.' Lucy
laughed hollowly.

'Yeah. Strong and silent and infuriating. And
I'm feeling a bit…battered.' Not just physically,
but emotionally, even though she had no right to
feel that at all.

But he'd never told her his true feelings about
their break-up or her infertility. He'd always been
an enigma. His expressions had betrayed his emotions, but he would refuse to talk about the way he
felt. Oh, he'd told her he loved her and cherished
her; about how much he'd cared; that he believed
in her, that she was amazing… But getting him
to talk about raw things, core-deep things? He'd
rather have stuck pins in his eyes. He'd thought it

was stoicism to keep quiet about difficult issues but in the end it was just intractability.

Was he married now? Had he a family of his own? Had he made it work with someone else? That thought hurt her too much for her to dwell on.

She looked at her little niece, fast asleep in her mother's arms, and her heart twinged.

'He held her, Lucy. He looked so right with a baby in his arms. It clarified everything—I did the right thing by leaving him so he could have that in his future. Even though he would never admit I did us both a favour.' It had almost broken her to see him hold Stella and remind her of the dreams they'd once shared. And she'd told him he was a natural parent. Oh, God, why had she said that? But she'd been so wrong-footed at seeing him, and him cooing over the baby, the words had tumbled out of her.

Lucy patted Charlie's arm. 'Oh, honey. I can imagine how it must have felt seeing him with a baby in his arms.'

'I think… I don't know if I managed to set him straight or not, it's all a bit blurry. But I think he believes Stella is *my* baby.'

'Yikes.' Her sister pulled a face. 'Awkward.'

'Very. It all seemed too much to explain all at once—why I'm here, who Stella belongs to and why she was in my car…your car. Your very wrecked car.' Charlie winced at the thought of dealing with all of the insurance stuff now. 'See?

It's a lot. Plus, I didn't want to tell him about your illness without checking in with you first. I know you're still coming to terms with it all and it's not common knowledge.'

'Tell whoever you like. It's not a secret. Except Mum and Dad, obviously. I'm not ready for their reaction yet. I need to be stronger for their panic than I feel right now.'

Their parents would drop everything if they knew Lucy was sick, even their dream trip. 'Okay, well, if it comes up I'll set Lewis straight about why I'm back.' To look after Lucy and Stella— not…repeat, *not*…to pine after the man she'd left. Or pine about what they'd once had before the sex on schedule, the failed pregnancy tests and the medical tests and scans.

Okay, enough now.

Time to put thought into action. She stood up and headed towards the kitchen. 'Right, then, let's get that tea made.'

'Thanks, hun.' Lucy grimaced. 'It's so weird, having you look after me.'

Charlie hovered in the kitchen doorway. 'Why?'

'Because I'm the older sister. I'm supposed to look after you.'

'You always have. Very well.' Too much, if she was being honest. There was eight years between Lucy and her, so she'd had a big sister to look out for her from day one. A very devoted big sister.

Born to older parents, Charlie had always felt

she might have been a 'Band-Aid' baby to help heal a possible rift between her mother and father. A child to make everyone happy again, another focus. And, given that Lucy had never wanted to follow in the family footsteps as a doctor, there'd been a lot of pressure on Charlie to fulfil her parents' expectations, and a lot of attending to Charlie's every need.

By the time she'd graduated from medical school, and then married and moved in with Lewis, she hadn't had a day living on her own or fighting her own battles—being herself. She'd always been Lucy's kid sister, the formidable Dr Rose's daughter, Lewis's wife. She'd been well taken care of but smothered too. It hadn't been until she'd settled on her own in London that she'd realised just how much she'd leaned into that.

Not any more. 'Sit back and rest; it's my turn to look after you.'

She'd deal with the Lewis problem later. *If* she could get him out of her head. But, after seeing him up close, having him touch her with such tenderness and care, getting him out of her head was proving a lot more difficult than she'd thought.

'Eighty-two-year-old gentleman: Henry Gerald Woods. Slipped on wet lino in the kitchen at home last night. Couldn't get himself back up and had to wait for his carers to come in this morning. Complaining of severe pain in his right hip.

Blood pressure eighty over fifty at presentation, now ninety-four over sixty-seven. Slightly hypothermic at thirty-four point nine degrees when found, rising steadily now. IV zero point nine percent normal saline in situ. Pain score eight out of ten initially, but has come down to five after morphine administration. We brought his medications in. Takes daily fluid tablets and beta blockers.' Lewis handed his patient's tablets over to the A and E triage nurse.

'Thanks, we'll take over from here,' she said, and smiled at Henry as they lifted him from the portable trolley onto the hospital gurney. 'Hello, Henry. Back again so soon? What on earth have you been up to this time?'

'See you, mate.' Lewis nodded at Henry, one of their 'frequent flyers' who insisted on independent living whilst also refusing to wear the alert necklace that would bring help quickly when needed. 'Don't go giving these lovely nurses any of your cheek, okay?'

'You're just jealous of my charisma,' Henry joked, just audible around the confines of his oxygen mask.

'To be fair, our man Lewis here has plenty of charisma. He just keeps it well hidden.' Brin laughed and opened the cubicle curtain for Lewis to step into the hustle and bustle of the A and E logistics area.

Lewis's heart immediately started its staccato

rhythm of anxiety and, unexpectedly, excitement. Was Charlie here? He glanced around the large open space. She was not at the work stations in the centre of the room; not obviously in the corridor. He couldn't hear her voice coming from one of the cubicles. Couldn't see her giveaway red locks.

Hot damn, he'd never been on the lookout for a glimpse of her and her gorgeous hair in here before. In fact, because she'd been doing her medical rotations when they'd been married, they'd never worked in the same department until now—today.

Yesterday, to be factually correct, but he'd earlier overheard one of the nurses saying that the new emergency doctor had been involved in a car crash and that she was mostly unharmed and had come back this morning. So far, he'd managed three visits here over his shift and he hadn't seen anything of her. Now he was clocking off, he could breathe again. The chances of seeing her now were slim to nil.

Until tomorrow. When he'd be on high alert all over again.

'Lewis?' Brin's tone was brisk and he was frowning. 'I said, do you want to go sort the van out and I'll grab us some takeaway coffees?'

'Sure.' The sooner he got out of here, the sooner he'd stop looking for her.

Brin's frown deepened. 'You seem a bit distracted today. You okay?'

'Never better.' Lewis nodded, determined to

stay focused on the job. He hadn't thought it nec-essary to tell Brin about his relationship status with the new emergency doctor, but no doubt he'd have to soon enough. 'Cheers, yes. Trim flat white, please, and one of those giant chocolate-chip cookies. Meet you at the van.'

Once in the ambulance bay, he took a deep breath of the fresh, sea-salted air and was just about to climb into the back of the van to tidy up when he caught a flash of red hair. A figure was walking towards the hospital entry, moving stiffly with her head down, right next to where he was standing.

She lifted her head. Their gazes tangled. *Damn.* Now she'd seen him, neither of them could avoid the inevitable, awkward small talk.

'Um… Hi, Lewis.' She inhaled as she ap-proached, a hesitant smile hovering on her lips.

And, damn it, if he couldn't help thinking about the way she tasted. *Don't. Just don't.*

Now there was no urgency of injury assess-ment or need to rescue, as there had been yes-terday, he was able to take a longer look at her. She was still achingly beautiful with her huge blue eyes, pale Celtic skin, that gorgeous kiss-able mouth and blush-pink lips. But she was thin-ner, her cheekbones more pronounced, and there were little lines around her eyes when she smiled. She hadn't done a lot of that with him in the later years of their marriage, but he'd seen them there yesterday when she'd hugged her baby. He swallowed. 'Hey, Charlotte.'

'*Charlotte?* Not Charlie?' A pause. Clearly, she was finding this as difficult as he was. 'Okay, yes. I guess we're at that point, right?'

Which point, exactly? They'd breached breaking point a long time ago. His gut clenched as he cleared his throat. 'I was just being polite.'

In truth, 'Charlie' was the woman he'd adored. Using her formal, full name 'Charlotte' gave him emotional space.

'I know…exactly. It's just, you never called me Charlotte.' She shook her head and her eyes darkened, as if she was carrying the world on her shoulders. 'Okay, so, while I have the chance, I want to thank you for what you did for me yesterday.'

'No problem. I was just doing my job. How are you?'

She shrugged her right shoulder and winced. 'Sore, as expected, and bruised. But I'll live.'

His innate immediate response was to put his arms round her and tell her to rest up, that he'd look after her, but they weren't in that space any more. Things between them had broken. Instead, he found what he hoped was a benign smile and said, 'So take it easy, okay? No heavy lifting.'

She nodded, her expression difficult to read. 'Okay. Thank you.'

He was just about to turn away but then had

another thought. 'And your baby—Stella? She's okay?'

Her features softened at the mention of Stella. She clearly loved her daughter very much. 'Yes, she's fine. No issues at all. In fact, I've just been to check on her at the hospital creche.'

Oh, God, this was all too painful. He needed not to be here with her. 'Good to hear. Right, well, I've got to get on, you know...'

'Wait, Lewis. I need to explain.' Her hand touched his wrist, stopping him from turning away. He felt warmth on his skin from a gesture that was almost too intimate. Her skin was soft, her grip light with delicate bones, beautiful hands. But he didn't, couldn't, draw attention to the gesture because that would make things even more awkward.

'No, look, you don't have to explain anything. It's not my business.' Nevertheless, the ache to know everything was surprising and deep. That Charlie had a family was a shock, and it wasn't just the 'who with?', but the *'how?'*.

She looked at her fingers on his and her eyes widened. Grimacing, she lifted her hand and shoved it into her scrubs pocket. 'Um... Stella isn't my baby. She's my niece—Lucy's daughter.'

'Ah.' *Okay*...he'd jumped to conclusions. Something in his chest shifted and eased a little. 'Okay.... Lucy. Of course, Lucy's baby. I see.'

Charlie shook her head. 'No, I don't think you

do. I've come home because Lucy is sick.' Her eyes flickered closed briefly as if she was finding it hard to say the words. 'Breast cancer.'

His gut knotted. 'God, I'm sorry. And with a young baby too. That's terrible. Is she…is she going to be okay?'

'It's early days with the chemo, but the odds are good. I'm helping her look after Stella, and of course I'm trying my best to look after Lucy too, but you might remember that that's not always easy.'

Of course; he remembered that the two sisters had had a difficult dynamic at times. Lucy had always been slightly domineering, a bit meddlesome but well intentioned. Charlie used to complain that her family was trying to be the third spoke in her marriage, in her life.

The Roses were a tight unit: a doting sister and helicopter parents. They'd always been in each other's business, with entangled lives…in a good way, mostly. He'd kind of envied them that closeness which was so very, very different from his own family. His parents had never lived in the same town, never mind the same house. He hadn't heard from his dad…ever. And he wasn't exactly sure where his nomad mother was; last time he'd heard, she was in Invercargill but planning to leave there because it was too cold. That was, what, six months ago? She wasn't great at keeping in touch, regardless of how many times he texted or called.

But at least he had a good bond with his twin brother, Logan. If Logan had been ill, Lewis would have done the same as Charlie and given up his life to look after his sibling. 'Of course I remember. You were joined at the hip growing up. Maybe she'll let you look after her, for a change. *Maybe?*'

'I wish.' Charlie seemed to relax a little, knowing he understood her dilemma. 'She's hellbent on doing everything, but she's so tired. Looking after a baby is knackering enough without cancer treatment too. But that's why I took a part-time job here—so I can fit my work around my life for a change. To be honest, I'd prefer not to be working at all while I look after her, but someone needs to pay the bills, right?'

'Right, of course. I hope she has a speedy recovery.' So Charlie hadn't had a sudden change of heart about her ex and rushed back for him. Not that he'd thought that but…maybe his pathetic heart had hoped? Yeah, he didn't want to admit to a fleeting hope. 'And your parents? Are they okay too?'

He had to ask, right? He couldn't exactly have a half-conversation about her family. But this was just about the most awkward he'd ever felt: asking guarded, polite questions about people he'd known, loved and spent many happy times with of the woman he'd rocked into; whose hair he'd held when she'd vomited after a fun night out and too many drinks; with whom he'd laughed; with whom he'd planned his whole life. Now she was like a stranger, with a completely different life.

'They're fine. Retired now, but doing charity work in Uganda. We haven't told them about Lucy's diagnosis because they'd rush back. You know what they're like; they need to be in the thick of our lives and it's a bit stifling. I can't tell you how relieved we were when they decided to travel, just doing things for themselves, you know? Lucy didn't want them to cut their time in Uganda short so I just told them I'd decided to come home for a while to spend time with my sister.'

She suddenly looked flustered, shaking her head and rolling her eyes. 'God, I don't know why I'm telling you all this. You're busy; you should probably go. What am I saying? I'm busy too. And I'm going to be late back to work. I'm sorry, Lewis.'

'Don't, Charlotte. Don't apologise.' He was amused by her fluster, glad she'd been able to let off some steam and talk about her sister's illness. 'Give my regards to Lucy.'

'I will. Thanks.' She looked a little relieved and smiled. Had she been worried about how this whole interaction would go? Had she thought he might bring up their past? Because, hell, there was a lot to unpick there. But maybe it was best to keep it firmly in the past.

He found himself smiling too, despite the weirdness of everything. 'Take care, Charlotte...um... Charlie. See you around.'

'Yes. Undoubtedly.' She smiled properly then, a full-blown mega-watt smile that did something to his chest. He hadn't realised just how much he'd been looking forward to seeing that smile again. How much the ache for her was still embedded in his DNA.

Then he watched her walk away.

The story of my life.

There was no way he'd let himself fall for her again. She'd broken his heart once and, if he wasn't careful, she could do it again.

CHAPTER FOUR

CHARLIE TOOK A seat at the empty round table in the fundraiser venue, not entirely happy to be here when she should have been at home looking after her sister and her niece. But Lucy had made her come, waving her off with a big smile, a sigh and a promise to call if she felt poorly.

'You need to get out more,' Lucy had said. 'You can't spend your whole life stuck within these four walls with me. You need some friends, Charlie.'

'I go out to work and to the supermarket,' Charlie had replied, as if grocery shopping was the most exciting thing in the world. 'I want to be here.'

'And I need you to go out. You're making me feel guilty, hogging you all the time when you should be building a social life now that you've come home. You're too young to be spending all your waking hours around sick people.' Lucy had smiled her wan smile and sighed. 'Go to that comedy night you were talking about the other day, have fun then come home and tell me all about it. I want to live a normal Saturday night vicariously.'

I need you to go out. Just like that, Charlie had read between the lines. Lucy was grateful to have

Charlie here to help, but spending all this time together was as stifling as their home had been growing up. Lucy wanted things to feel normal instead of staring down the barrel of sickness and uncertainty. So here Charlie was, hoping the comedy part of the night would give her something to laugh about so she could retell it all to Lucy and make her giggle too.

A chatting, laughing group of people entered the large events centre and scanned the room for their table. Charlie recognised them: Patience and Arno, two staff nurses from work, followed by a couple of junior doctors who had recently joined the team, Seung and Mei. Charlie stood up and waved. 'Here! We're over here.'

Patience waved back and started to make her way over with the doctors, while Arno nodded, then turned to speak to people behind him: a woman she didn't know, who was holding hands with one of the paramedics that seemed to spend their life in the A and E department, and behind them…

Lewis.

No. Her belly tightened.

No.

Charlie slid down in her seat. Did the Emergency department have so few people keen to make up a table of eight that they'd had to invite the visiting paramedics too? The last thing she wanted to do was spend the evening with him.

That had been her normal once upon a time but it wasn't now. Hadn't been for five years and, judging by the way her body prickled at the sight of him, her instinctive reaction at seeing him was one of excitement and anticipation.

No. Please, no. She was supposed to be building a new life. Despite him being nice to her, he was probably just being polite. He probably hated her. He probably had a wife and kids.

How to act with him in the company of colleagues and friends? Did they acknowledge they knew each other more than people thought they did, or pretend they were strangers?

She patted the space next to her and indicated to Patience to come and sit down. But she wasn't quick enough, embroiled as she was in air kisses with her colleagues, to see that all the seats were being taken except for the one on the other side of her. And there was only one person left still standing.

'Lewis, hi.' She gave him a tight smile. 'Looks like this is your seat.'

'This is awkward,' he whispered, as if feeling her embarrassment. 'Sorry. There isn't anywhere else.'

So he was approaching this head-on. She nodded, her throat tight. 'It's okay. I'm sure we can get through one evening.'

'Of course. I don't think anyone here knows about our past so let's just keep it that way, right?

Let's just forget about everything and try have a good time.' He caught her gaze and...*oh, dear*... those brown eyes had her all tangled up inside.

Forget everything? What was he saying? She could never forget being married to Lewis: their courtship, the wedding, the dreamy honeymoon, the laughter, the fun...the sex. *Oh*, the sex.

But it wasn't meant to be. They'd tried to make it work and failed. She'd walked away in the end, desperate for some space from the sadness of it all. She'd left him, taken a job on the other side of the world, and the guilt of doing that still stung. Should she have stayed and tried harder? Could they have worn the difficulties they'd faced if they'd stuck it through? He probably did hate her, but how would she know? He'd agreed they separate, but he hadn't told her how he felt about any of it.

So what could she do now but agree to keep everything civil? Just civil, as if they were mere colleagues. She nodded. 'Sure. I don't want to bring the mood down either. Deal.'

'Drink?' He reached for one of the bottles of wine on the table and hovered it over her glass.

'Absolutely. Thanks.'

Lewis poured their drinks and sat down, his knee knocking against hers. He grimaced and shifted away but she was left with his scent lingering in the air: his favourite cologne and something that was uniquely Lewis. It was as familiar to her as her morning coffee aroma.

But she needn't have worried about any further awkwardness because he was immediately embroiled in a conversation with Dr Mei beside him. And Patience engaged Charlie in a conversation about the emergency department politics then introduced her to the other paramedic, Brin—of whom she'd seen lots but didn't know—and his girlfriend Mia.

Apparently Mia was a nurse practitioner at a local GP practice. She told Charlie that Brin was Irish but had settled here now. They had a little girl called Harper. They spent half their lives on Rāwhiti Island and they'd recently been there with the guy sitting next to her—Lewis. Did Charlie know him?

Remembering their deal, Charlie simply nodded at that and redirected her conversation to their holiday with him. *Had he been there with a significant other—a wife, girlfriend?* Of course she didn't ask that, even though she was suddenly very keen to know the answer. Had he found someone else? She tried to read between the conversation lines…she was getting good at that these days… but it was just *Lewis this, Lewis that…*

He was such good fun, apparently: a talented fisherman; a good friend; a dab hand at the barbecue; great with kids. He babysat their daughter sometimes. He was a real good guy.

Her heart felt raw. She knew that, of course,

more than any of them. A good guy with a heart of gold...

Eventually Lewis rolled his eyes at Brin and told him to stop with the ego massaging but Brin just grinned. 'Ah, man. I'm just telling Charlie here how it is.' Brin turned back to her. 'I see you're here on your own tonight, Charlie. Do you have a partner? Family?'

They all looked at her then and her mouth felt as dry as a husk. 'Um... No to both—'

'What is this?' Lewis interrupted, jumping to her aid like he used to, his voice imbued with humour, but Charlie knew him better. Knew it was forced. 'I'm sure Charlie doesn't need an interrogation.'

Brin shrugged and shot his friend a curious look. 'Being friendly, is all. Getting to know the new doc in town.'

Charlie didn't need Lewis's help any more. She'd grown up a lot while she'd been in London and could fight her own battles. She smiled at them both. 'No worries at all. I've no partner, no kids. I'm from Auckland but I've been away for a few years. Now I'm back.'

'And we're glad to have you.' Brin raised his glass and looked at Lewis. He made some sort of face, pigging his eyes at him as if to encourage him to say something.

Lewis shook his head tightly... There was something going on between these two—some in joke or something. In the end, Lewis cleared his throat and said almost robotically, 'Hey. Yes. We're glad you're here.'

Yet she didn't think he was glad at all. He didn't want anyone to know about their shared past. He'd physically shifted away from her when he'd sat down. He'd glared at any suggestion of being too friendly towards her.

The lights dimmed and the comedienne took to the stage. She was funny, and told some great stories that almost distracted Charlie from the fact she was sitting here in the dark next to her ex-husband who clearly wanted to be anywhere but next to her. But they were all crammed in round the table. He was so close, and she was acutely aware of him. Once upon a time they'd have held hands at an event like this, played footsie under the table. He'd have slid his arm around the back of her chair, absentmindedly playing with her hair or massaging her shoulder. She'd have leant into him and he'd have kissed the top of her head.

Even now his leg kept pressing against hers as they shifted position in their seats, but that was more because they'd been shunted together than by desire. But she was wrapped in his scent, mesmerised by his hands as they played with the stem of his wine glass. She'd always loved his hands and his long, slender fingers.

Her gaze roamed the place where his wedding band had once sat. They'd bought their rings from a high street chain because they hadn't been able to afford anything too swanky. But they'd loved their choices—a simple band for him and stacked engagement and wedding rings for her. There wasn't even a white line on his finger any more. Time and the sun had filled in the place where his ring used to be.

She looked at her own hands then. Her wedding-ring finger was empty too; there were no tan lines around where the platinum ring had been. It was all so long ago. She'd kept the rings, though, at the bottom of her jewellery box. There'd been something so desperately sad about getting rid of them. Even after the divorce had come through, she kept them as a reminder that once she'd been in love and been loved. That she'd planned an idyllic future…until the dream had fallen apart due to her damned useless uterus.

It was a great relief when, during the interval, they were all encouraged to bid on items in a silent auction. Charlie jumped up and took some well-needed breathing space, walking down the side of the room, reading the details of the silent-auction items. She wrote her name and her bid on a few of them, then made her way back to her seat. The table was empty and she could see most of her colleagues standing in a queue to bid in the auction too.

But where was…? 'Hey.'

Ah. Lewis was here, taking his seat next to her

again. His tone was flat, as if he was pushing himself to talk to her and fill in the yawning conversational gap.

'Hi.' She turned to speak to him and smiled to try and soften the atmosphere. 'I managed to bid on a few things—a couple of spa packages for Lucy for when she's feeling up to having some nice treatments, and the paddling pool for Stella. You?'

'I'm sure Lucy would love to be pampered when she's up to it.' He shrugged. 'There's not much there for guys, to be honest, but I'm bidding on the dinner at that fancy restaurant, Marcel's.'

'Is it good? I'm a bit out of the loop when it comes to restaurants here.'

'I don't know.' He gave another shrug. 'I've been wanting to try it for a while.'

'Oh.' Fleetingly she wondered whether he was planning to take a date there. And then her competitive streak got the better of her. 'Well, I was the last one to bid on that, so don't you dare outbid me.'

His eyebrows rose. And there…just there…she saw a glimpse of the old Lewis in the glimmer of a smile playing across his lips and the spark of tease. 'Or…what?'

'Or…' She jumped up, throwing him a gauntlet she thought he might not refuse, because he never could resist a dare. 'I'll just have to bid higher than you.'

'Not likely.' He jumped up too and started towards the table that held the restaurant auction. And just like that they were back seven years playing, competing, laughing.

'Don't you dare, Lewis Parry!' She dashed ahead of him but he scooted in front of her as they both arrived at the table at the same time. They reached out, their hands entwining as their fingers curled round the pen. For the briefest moment, she felt a skitter of electricity through her skin, arrowing towards her heart. But she wasn't going to let go of the pen for love nor money.

'Mine!' He looked at her, pulling a face and laughing. 'Mine. Mine.'

Back in the halcyon days of their relationship, they'd watched *Finding Nemo* and had laughed so hard at the seagull scene where the birds fought for fish shouting, 'Mine, mine, mine!' Every time they'd seen a seagull after that, they'd mimicked the word over and over, dissolving into fits of laughter.

Her heart flooded with something… Nostalgia, or just muscle memory? She laughed at his victorious expression: *I win.* 'I think not, Mr Parry. *Mine.* I was here first.'

'Hey hey, children. Now, now.' A voice behind them made them jump apart.

They turned to see Brin grinning at them both. 'This is for charity, it's not WWE wrestling. Truce?'

They looked at each other and she saw Lewis trying to stifle more laughter as much as she was. In the end, she couldn't hold it in, and chuckled. 'We were a bit petty, weren't we?'

'Nothing like a bit of healthy competition.' Lewis grinned back. 'I'm still going to beat you.'

'Not a chance, Lewis. Not a chance.'

Brin looked from one to the other, frowning at first, but the frown slowly dissolved as the moments ticked by. He was clearly cooking up something. 'I have an idea—hear me out. It's not guaranteed that either of you will win, cos there are plenty of others bidding on this auction too, but if one of you does win…why don't you share the prize?'

'What?' Charlie and Lewis said to Brin at the same time, both wide-eyed.

'Genius, yes?' Brin laughed.

Charlie could think of other words to describe the suggestion: meddlesome, idiotic, dangerous. If she was spending this evening looking at Lewis's wedding-ring finger, and trying to prise information out of him when he clearly wasn't interested, then she needed to spend less time with him, not more.

Hell, she wasn't interested in her ex-husband… was she?

No. Working with him was just a new dynamic she had to get used to. She'd need to work out a new normal. Besides, someone else could easily outbid them. She looked at Brin, then at Lewis, and they both stared back expectantly. And now she couldn't exactly say no, could she? That would just seem rude. 'Okay…maybe.'

'Oh.' Lewis scrunched his nose as he thought—playful Lewis replaced again with the earlier, more detached one. 'Well. Um… I guess…maybe too.'

Huh. Don't hold back on the enthusiasm, matey. His reluctance bit deep.

Brin nodded. 'Nice. Good. I'll take that as two yesses.'

Now was her chance to find out Lewis's relationship status. She looked up at him. 'Shouldn't you check with your partner first?'

Lewis frowned, confused, then he shook his head and threw Brin a wry look. 'This is all your fault, *partner*. So, I'm not asking permission. I may well kill you later, though.'

Yikes. But he was at least smiling a little. So perhaps he didn't find the prospect of dinner with her so odious. And…was that Lewis's way of telling her he was single? Okay, dinner might be a good idea—maybe they could clear the air and stop all this awkwardness around them whenever they met.

They wandered back to their table and the evening continued, but Charlie was a little blindsided about what she'd just agreed to. She couldn't get it out of her head: dinner with Lewis?

Dinner with Lewis…after everything they'd

been through? After their divorce? What in the actual hell had she been thinking when she'd said yes?

The comedienne finally started going through the silent auction and announcing the winners. Charlie stood and waved at the applause for her generous bid on one of the spa packages. She also won the paddling pool for Stella.

Then came the announcement for dinner at Marcel's. The comedienne cleared her throat. 'Now for the last auction item of the night. We're very lucky to have Marcel, the restaurant owner, here with us tonight. His father was an in-patient at the hospital a couple of weeks ago, and Marcel was so impressed with the care given that he has decided to add an extra-special treat for the person who wins the bid for dinner at his restaurant…'

'Ooh? Wonder what it is?' Brin gave Lewis and Charlie a thumbs-up. 'Maybe a bottle of champagne too?'

She shook her head. 'Won't be me. I'm never that lucky.'

Lewis laughed. 'Well, I'm always up for a free bottle of champagne.'

'Not just dinner…but also a night for two in the luxury of the Quay Hotel. Time for some rest and relaxation or…' the comedienne winked suggestively '…whatever you fancy doing in a very swanky hotel for the night. I know I wouldn't want to just sleep between those eight-hundred-thread-count sheets…'

Charlie glanced at Lewis. He was looking right at her.

A night in a hotel…together…between the sheets. Something inside her flickered to life. And something in his eyes told her he was thinking the same thing. His gaze softened yet heated at the same time. She knew that look. She had basked in it many, many times. His eyes were molten and, in return, her insides melted. Heat shot through her. Her body thrummed.

One night with him…

He was so close. Close enough to touch, to kiss. And she'd seen the old Lewis a few moments ago, laughing and playing, uninhibited by disappointment or sadness. She had a sudden ache to run her fingers across his jaw, to press her mouth against his.

Whoa. Really? But then, the physical side of their relationship had never been the problem. Their desire for each other had been insatiable.

Did he feel the same need?

No. No. No.

He looked away and shook his head, as if giving himself a good telling off. *So maybe, yes, yes, yes?* He had been thinking the same thing!

The ache inside her intensified. She ran her fingers round the stem of her wine glass, hoping the cool condensation would bring her some relief. Hoping like hell that neither of them won that prize.

'And the winner of this amazing prize is… Drum roll, please…' The whole room erupted with people banging the tables. 'Lewis Parry!'

'Oh?' His chest inflated as he sucked in air. His eyebrows rose and then he nodded at her. 'Okay. Okay, looks like we're doing this.'

She watched him walk across the room with his long legs and confident stride. The years had been good to him; he looked fitter, stronger, even more gorgeous.

And so off-limits.

She'd broken everything. It had been her fault, in the end. Doing the right thing by him had meant breaking her own heart too. But she cheered as he stepped onto the stage and shook hands with the famous Marcel.

He collected the vouchers, chatted with some other members of the audience then returned to the table as everyone was starting to put on coats to leave. The night was over.

He helped her with her denim jacket and then handed her the hotel information. 'Hey, you can have the hotel room, I don't want it.'

She looked down at the pamphlet. It was indeed a very fine-looking place and, oh, so tempting.

'No thanks. I'll need to be back for Lucy, in case she needs me. You take it.'

'No, Charlie. You should take it. You're doing a lot for your sister; you deserve a good night's sleep.'

'If you don't take it, I'll give it away.' She laughed. 'Maybe to your partner in crime?'

His gaze flicked to Brin, ahead of them in the crowd milling towards the exit, and he laughed. 'Not a chance. He doesn't know about our past. I think he was trying to…you know…'

'Get us together?' She watched Lewis's reaction. 'Bit of a stirrer?'

He shook his head, a little guarded, and rolled his eyes. 'He's got a good sense of humour, for sure. One of these days it's going to get him into trouble. Right, I'll book the restaurant. Friday? Saturday? I can do either. I'm on early shifts this week.'

With a roll of his eyes, he showed he was clearly still reluctant. And yet they were planning a dinner out. 'Feel free to take someone else, Lewis.'

'Oh, no, you don't. You had a deal,' chipped in Brin, who had obviously overheard bits of their conversation. 'Both of you go, or I'll take Mia. I do love a free dinner, and a hotel room. You can babysit instead of a lovely meal. Yes, please.'

'Funny guy.' Lewis flicked his thumb towards Brin and shook his head. Then he leaned closer to Charlie and lowered his voice. 'Truth is, I only bid one cent more than you anyway.'

'What? You little…' She laughed and gasped at the whisper of his breath across her skin. 'Anything to win, right?'

'You know me.' His eyebrows rose and he stopped walking.

'I certainly do.' Her gaze landed on his mouth and joy fizzed through her as she watched him laugh. It was so refreshing, so damned lovely to see. She'd missed it, missed him. Missed *them*. Oh, God. She hadn't realised how confusing seeing him again, being with him, would be.

Maybe they needed this dinner to clear the air. *Yes—excellent idea.* 'I'm on call Friday night but Saturday works. Then you can have a nice lie-in on Sunday morning in your swanky hotel room— not that I'd be jealous at all.'

Sunday morning—their favourite time for sex. Long, lazy mornings in bed on the rare occasions they'd both had Sundays off. It was a ritual they'd enjoyed almost until the end—uncomplicated, leisurely, exploring each other. She remembered the touch of his fingers and the press of his body on her, over her, inside her…the way he'd tasted. Her body tingled in awareness. He was still so damned close.

His breath hitched and he cleared his throat, and she was fairly sure he was remembering all their Sunday mornings too.

'Cool,' he said. 'Saturday it is.'

Which meant she had precisely one week to stop thinking about Lewis in bed. And to start thinking of him as purely and only her colleague.

CHAPTER FIVE

SO OUT OF NOWHERE, and after five years apart, he was going out to dinner with his ex-wife—*tomorrow*.

If anyone had told him last week, last month or even last year he'd be doing this, he'd have laughed in their face. But, yeah, dinner.

He was finishing up a few days on early shift so hadn't seen much of Charlie, except in passing in the corridor and twice at a patient handover surrounded by the team—certainly not long enough for a chat.

It had given him enough time to put some well-needed space and perspective on the whole thing. Dinner was a good idea. A chance to catch up on everything and smooth the transition from not seeing each other for a very long time to working together a few times a week. To work out how to be, with her back in his life. It wasn't as if he could avoid it, so he needed a plan to get through it.

He wandered across the hospital ambulance shared car park towards his car, planning a quick ride home, a speedy shower and then heading to his niece's birthday party.

'Lewis!' A female voice behind him had him turning round.

He spotted luscious red curls coming towards him, bobbing between the cars: *Charlie*, her hand raised in a wave.

His heart did a weird leap as all the perspective faded away and he was back to the other night, imagining her in bed. In his bed, for Sunday morning sex—his favourite time of the week.

He couldn't have stopped the smile if he'd tried. 'Hey, we have to stop meeting like this.' *Yeah. Corny as hell.*

'I know, right? Who would have thought the work car park would be our new rendezvous place?' She laughed, but her smile was sad and her eyes were red-rimmed.

His gut knotted the way it always did when Charlie was anything other than happy, as if it was his own personal mission to put a smile back on her face.

But that had been before. Now, he needed to keep some emotional distance before he got all bent out of shape with trying to make her happy. That wasn't his job any more. She'd walked away, but not before telling him he needed to focus on himself and not on her. That she didn't want or need his platitudes.

But, still, she looked upset and he couldn't ignore that. 'You okay?'

She shrugged, her eyes weary. 'Sure.'

She didn't look okay at all. He nodded towards the creche. 'Just been to see Stella?'

'Actually, just on my way to pick her up. I'm done working for the day.'

'And she's okay?' At her nod, he frowned. 'So, what's up? You look upset.'

'Oh, I'm just tired.' She waved her hand wearily in front of her face. 'Lucy had a bad night with pain and vomiting. She refuses to let me get up if Stella wakes, but she's so weak after her chemo, so I make sure to get up too. For some reason, Stella was agitated just after midnight, and around two-thirty, and then again at four-eighteen precisely. Not that I was clock-watching.' She rolled her eyes.

'Could be teething. Is she drooling more than usual? Pink cheeks?' Then he smacked his head with his palm. 'Duh. You're talking to a doctor, Lewis.'

She laughed. 'Always happy for advice. What do you know about teething?'

'Logan had hellish sleepless nights with both Lily and Lola, remember?'

'Oh, yes, of course. I'd forgotten about your brother's kids. We babysat them that time and couldn't calm Lily down at all. I thought she didn't like me.'

'She loved you.'

We all did.

His heart twinged. When Charlie had fled to London, she'd left a hole in his family. She'd not just been his wife, but an auntie and sister-in-law too. He hadn't told Logan she was back…that was going to be an interesting conversation. 'Teething—a whole new dynamic to test you, just when you think you're getting into a routine.'

Charlie chuckled. 'Yes, it's probably just her teeth coming through. She's definitely unsettled. I hope she's not feeding off our worries over Lucy's diagnosis. Kids are funny like that.'

'Sure are. Logan used to cool teething rings and let them suck on them. Said it worked a treat.' It made him sad to think they could talk about other people's child-rearing woes but not their own. And he knew damned well just how much a parent's anxiety, worry or neglect could have an effect. He'd lived it, breathed it. His mother had barely hidden her struggles with her twin sons.

You ruined my life. I could have been something if you two hadn't come along.

Of course, looking back, he knew it had been more her struggles with her own mental health than anything to do with their behaviour, but at the time it had been devastating. 'I'm sure you're doing all the right things to shield her from any upset.'

Charlie sighed. 'Oh, I hope so. But it's a vicious circle sometimes. If Lucy's upset, then Stella seems more grizzly. And of course if Stella's awake, then so is Lucy. And so am I. I've come to work for the rest.' She laughed wryly.

'It's a lot.'

'It certainly is. I'm never going to admit it to Lucy, because she needs my help, not my gripes, but I didn't realise babies were such hard work.' She pressed her lips together, wincing. 'Oh… sorry.'

Her eyes caught his and their shared past flickered into view.

He recalled the doctor's gentle words. *I'm so sorry, but it is impossible for you to carry a child. There may be other options you could explore…*

It embarrassed Lewis to admit it now, but he hadn't wanted to consider other options back then. His whole focus had been to try to stop Charlie from hurting, hiding his own grief at losing his dream of being a father and helping her get through: throwing the bundle of unused pregnancy tests away when she wasn't looking; deleting the ovulation app from her phone; helping her in the way he'd *thought* she'd needed to be helped and giving no attention to the fact he needed help too. Of course, she'd noticed these things missing and had called him out, saying he needed to face his own grief and not try to protect her from hers.

And, in hindsight, he wondered whether this had tipped her over the edge, pushed her into her decision to leave.

He shook his head. 'It's fine, honestly. But, yes, I've heard the first six months are the worst. Until the second six months.' He chuckled.

She groaned. 'Gee, you're filling me with confidence.'

'Hey, you'll cope. Just like when you did your medical rotations and had those horrific weekends on call.' He winked, knowing how she'd managed to work but had been too exhausted to do anything else at the end of the weekends. He'd been the cook, the cleaner and the cheerleader. Hell, he'd always been her cheerleader…until it hadn't worked for her any more. She hadn't wanted to hear how much he loved her, how things were going to be okay, because they'd both known they weren't. 'But with a new job, a sick sister plus a grizzly baby: that's a triple whammy.'

'All the while you just fake it till you make it, right?' She flashed a fake smile, then a real one. Her eyes lit up and she just glowed. Or it could have been the way the setting sun lit up her face and hair in golden hues.

Either way, she was still so beautiful—older now but no less stunning. Just looking at her made his heart swell and his body prickle. He swallowed, trying to dampen the tingles firing across his skin and the tightening in his groin. 'And we are champion fakers, right? You remember Matt and Claire's wedding?'

'Oh, hell, yes. The traffic down to Tauranga was terrible. We were so late for the wedding that we met the bride and groom as they were coming out of the chapel…married.' She pulled a face: *woops.*

'And we pretended we'd watched the whole ceremony.' He laughed at the memory, parroting the way they'd greeted the new Mr and Mrs Sinclair. *'Congratulations, lovely service.'*

'Lovely service...' She laughed, putting on a cute, posh English accent. *'Just lovely.* They never knew we hadn't seen any of it and were just throwing confetti like we'd been there the whole time.'

'Faking pros, see? You can do it. You've got this.' Words he'd said over and over to her, from when they'd first started dating in the final year of school until that very last day when she'd told him she absolutely couldn't do it any more. That she *hadn't* got this. She didn't have a functioning uterus. She didn't have a child-filled future. She had no answers. That he was blinkered and no amount of positivity would get them through.

But he'd always believed in her. She believed she could do anything. And when her belief in herself had withered, he'd soldiered on, bolstering her up, thinking that was the way to show his love. Because that was what had always been missing in his life: no one had ever the hell said it to him. Not his mother, not the many random relatives they'd been sent to stay with in the school holidays and not even his brother.

But Charlie...yeah. She'd never actually said it when they'd been together but he'd always *felt* her belief in him: bone-deep; soul-deep.

Until she'd left.

He shook his head, coming back to reality with a bump. Because if thoughts about what she'd done to him weren't a warning call, he didn't know what was. He should have left then. He could have made an excuse and gone—hell, he was going to be late for Lola's birthday tea and that would not go down well with his brother.

But Charlie was still laughing and, he now realised, he was still acutely drawn to her, circling her like she was the goddamned sun.

'So don't be surprised if I fall asleep in my soup tomorrow night,' she quipped.

'Charming.' He fake-coughed. 'I hope my conversation is a little more riveting than that.'

'Well, I didn't want to say, but…' she joked, one eyebrow raised, her mouth all cocky and impudent as she fake-yawned.

And did she step closer? She was fingertip-distance away. He could see the flecks of silver in her eyes. The freckles she hated and he'd always loved. The laughter on her mouth and at the corners of her eyes. His first love—right here.

'You called me a lot of things over the years, Charlie Jade Rose.' He grinned and his gaze connected with hers. 'But boring was never one of them.'

'No.' She squared up to him, capturing his gaze, her pupils dilating and softening. Something white-hot fired there, igniting something scalding inside him. 'Definitely not boring.'

She was looking at him the way she had last week at the comedy night, eyes misted, body tilting towards him, all turned on and trembling. He *knew* that look. He knew her, and what she wanted.

Did she want him? Was he imagining it?

Did she want…?

He took a breath, but couldn't get enough oxygen into his lungs and drew his eyes away from hers. Everything was getting tangled up inside him. He looked away, then back. This time his gaze landed on her mouth. He wanted to kiss her. How the hell could he want to kiss her, after everything? But…he did. It was like an ache that had never really abated, only now rekindled, a hundred times more intense.

He took a step back before he did something stupid, like reach out and slide his mouth over hers. 'Look, I should go…'

'Sure.' But she didn't move.

How did a person greet and leave an ex-wife? Especially when there was this atmosphere of heat. There had been so much intimacy shared before, and now there was this five-year fissure. But they'd straddled it a little and were forging something like a collegial relationship at worst, a friendship at best.

Okay, he was freaking turned on as all hell. Should he give her a hug or an air-kiss goodbye?

A nod didn't seem enough. A hug would be too much…for him.

He leaned to kiss her cheek, trying to be platonic when platonic was not the way he felt.

The touch of his mouth on her skin sent his pulse into orbit. She smelt insanely delicious, and it felt as if her cheek was pressing against his mouth rather than the other way round. Maintaining skin contact, she turned her cheek until her mouth was centimetres from his.

His whole body buzzed. He should have moved back, away from her touch, but he couldn't.

'Lewis…' It was more of a tremble than a word and it connected with his gut, his groin, his skin, throbbing and beating inside him until the world around them faded to nothing and all he could see was her face—so compassionate, so beautiful, so familiar. *Charlie*…

And he couldn't have stopped it if he'd tried. He slid his fingers into her silken hair, cupped the back of her neck and slid his mouth softly over hers.

She shivered and moaned, her body trembling under his touch. Her eyes flickered closed. Her breath stuttered.

'Lewis…' she whispered against his mouth. 'I missed you.'

'*God,* Charlie. I never stopped missing you.' That was the truth of it.

He pulled her against him, relishing the press of

her body against his. Two pieces of a jigsaw slotting neatly and perfectly together. She raised her arms and framed his face with her hands, deepening the kiss. She tasted of fresh air and salty tears. Of Charlie from five years ago and something new...something intoxicating and exciting. There was no re-learning; it was as if they'd never stopped kissing. Had never had those five years apart.

His tongue slid into her mouth and she whimpered, which set him aflame. He wanted her, right here in the damned car park. But she pulled away and looked at him, her chest heaving. She just stared at him, her face a mix of sadness, surprise and heat. In those dark-blue eyes, he saw need and desire and he thought of all the things he wanted to do to her, with her, right now.

She opened her mouth to speak but his phone beeped.

He jumped and checked his phone: Logan. Could Lewis pick up some ice on the way over to the tea party?

Man, he loved his brother, but his timing was diabolical.

Although, also very wise.

Charlie was now studying her phone too as if she couldn't quite look him in the eye. Hell. What were they doing? The kiss was one road they should not have gone down. But then she shoved her phone into her bag and put her hand on his chest, looking up at him as if she was as confused as he was, and aching to be kissed again.

He shook his head and stepped well away. 'No. No. Just no, Charlie. We can't do this. *I* can't do this.'

Because he had to save them both here. They'd broken the good thing they'd once had. It could not be fixed back together with a kiss or a wish. It had taken him years to come to terms with his part in it all, get over her and move on.

She stepped back too, her expression half-regret and half-relief, but she was trembling as much as he was. 'Right. Yes. Okay. I've got to get Stella.'

He nodded, torn between wanting a repeat kiss and stopping this craving dead.

In the end, self-preservation won out. Once upon a time, she'd told him he had to stop putting her needs before his.

She was damned right.

And this time it was he who walked away and didn't look back.

CHAPTER SIX

DO NOT KISS HIM. Do not kiss him.

Lewis had made it very clear yesterday that kissing was not on his agenda and, while it stung… because it had been the most amazing kiss…he was right. Kissing was not a good idea.

But, hell, it had been inevitable. From the moment Charlie had seen him again after five years, she'd been assaulted by conflicting emotions— some sad, some funny, most hot—all about him and what they'd once had and lost. But the attraction was very much still there, simmering between them the way it always had.

But that was yesterday. Today, she'd convinced herself that they'd both needed some closure for the old part of their lives and the kiss had been the final full-stop on that.

So why they were still meeting up at Marcel's, she didn't know, but neither of them had cancelled so it appeared it was all still on. Well, he had paid an arm and a leg for it, so she guessed he didn't want to lose his money. As for her, well, it would be rude not to turn up after she'd agreed to accompany him as a friend. Besides, they really did need to get their relationship into civil territory, for a more congenial working environment as much as anything else.

And, of course, it was raining, with the promise of worse to come. Her umbrella had blown inside out twice since she'd climbed out of the taxi so now she was just holding it all limp and dripping above her head in a feeble attempt to keep maybe one strand of hair dry. But, as she approached the restaurant and caught her reflection in the window, she knew even that hadn't worked. Her trench coat was not, in fact, as advertised, waterproof. Her hair, which had been expertly and beautifully clipped up into a loose bun by her sister, was a flattened soggy mess, and her eyeliner and mascara were probably running down her face.

Lewis was standing in the restaurant doorway, hands shoved deeply into his jacket pockets, collar turned up, looking immaculate and, somehow, dry. He met her gaze with a little warmth—probably because he was resigned to coming tonight, so was making an effort to be cordial. 'Hey, Charlie. Quick, come inside; this weather is nuts.'

There was no kiss this time, not even an air-kiss. But he held the door open, she stepped inside the warm restaurant and was immediately assailed by the aroma of garlic, anise and something else exotic and delicious.

She shook her cold, wet hands and grimaced as water pooled at her feet. 'Ugh, sorry. Okay, I'm just heading to the bathroom to dry off. I must look a wreck.'

'No. You look amaz…' He swallowed and shook his head, taking her umbrella from her and putting it in a receptacle at the door. 'Okay, sure, of course. I'll find the table.'

Glumly, she stared at herself in the bathroom mirror. She'd been right: her hair needed drying and redoing and her mascara was now just two black smudges beneath her eyes—pretty much exactly the way she'd looked the day she'd left him. She'd been down and out, bedraggled, beaten up by elements out of her control. At least, that was how she'd felt back then.

But for some reason she wanted to show him, and show herself, that she'd put those days behind her. She was a different person from the one who'd gone to London. She was independent, capable and well put together…usually. She'd come to terms with her infertility and divorce, even though both stung when she dwelt on them too much. So she didn't dwell on them. There was no point looking back.

And yet here she was, looking back, going back. Wasn't it a sign of madness, repeating the same thing and expecting a different result? But this was just two friends catching up. That was all. No kissing allowed.

She quickly dried her hair under the hand drier, reapplied her make-up and slicked on her favourite lip gloss: *his* favourite lip gloss. *Whatever.* She just hadn't got round to finding one she liked better. *Honestly.* Well, you kept some things out of habit, right? And others purely for nostalgia.

She found him at a table overlooking the road and, beyond, the harbour. Water ran down the outside of the windows, distorting the reflections of people rushing through the early evening, car lights were fuzzy and the occasional blare of a car horn reminded her that driving in an Auckland downpour was dangerous.

As if she needed reminding about the dangers of cars. She rubbed her shoulder where the bruising was starting to fade from purple to yellow. Relaxing was difficult: not because she was in pain, but because she didn't know what to say or how to act. This felt intimate and yet disparate. They'd never been short on conversation before and now she was racking her mind, trying to think of the right things to say.

Trying not to think of that kiss.

Lewis frowned as he watched her movements. 'Does your shoulder hurt? Are you okay?'

'Oh, I'm fine, honestly. It's not so bad.' She rotated her shoulder forward and back to show him her range of movement. 'I was just thinking how nice and cosy it is in here, compared to outside.'

'There's flash-flooding forecast.' He laughed and then grimaced. 'I bet that's not easy to say after a couple of wines.'

'Flash flooding forecast,' she repeated, grateful that he'd broken the atmosphere with a joke. 'Maybe we should have some wine and see?'

As if on cue, Marcel appeared and shook their hands. 'Thank you, thank you, for bidding so much on the auction for the degustation dinner for two…'

What did he mean, *so much*? She glanced at Lewis for clarification. But Lewis just bugged his eyes at her to be quiet.

Marcel continued, 'I will throw in the wine match as a token of thanks.'

Lewis shook his head and smiled at the restaurant owner. 'Not necessary, honestly.'

'I insist.' Marcel reached for a bottle in an ice-bucket he'd brought with him and poured them a glass each of champagne. 'Bubbles to start. Are we celebrating anything tonight?'

They stared at each other.

Awkward.

How did they label this?

'Not really. Just—just two…um…old *friends*,' Lewis stammered, echoing the sudden panic inside her.

Old friends who happened to have been married and divorced. Old friends who had shared a searing hot kiss yesterday.

Marcel beamed. 'Well, old friends, have an excellent evening.'

Once he'd gone, Charlie leaned forward and whispered to Lewis, 'You said you'd paid one cent more than me. But I know I probably didn't bid enough to cover the cost of the meal.'

'Well, I may have embroidered the truth a little. All in a good cause—it's for the hospital cancer unit, right?' He sat back and regarded her, his arms casually crossed. His sultry gaze reached into her soul and something inside her flipped and danced. He'd always had a knack of disarming her just by looking at her. 'How are you doing, Charlie? I mean, *really*—how are you?'

She inhaled and thought about everything she was juggling at the moment and how it all seemed far away from here and now. 'I'm okay, I think. Yes, I'm good.'

'Good. Because I know you're under a lot of pressure.'

'It's nothing I can't handle.' She flashed him a wry smile because only yesterday she'd been bleating on about how it was all so difficult. But today she felt as if she could manage her way through being a decent sister, a good auntie and an efficient and compassionate doctor.

He smiled. 'You had a better sleep last night?'

'After we gave Stella the cooled teething ring, which worked like magic—thanks for the tip—we slept all night.' Apart from replaying that mind-warping kiss over and over before she'd fallen asleep, and immediately on waking.

His eyes flitted to her mouth and she wondered if he was remembering their kiss too or whether he'd put it to the back of his mind. She'd tried, but it was here now at the front, and she couldn't stop thinking about it.

He cleared his throat. 'Do we…um…need to talk about yesterday?'

Ah, so he had been thinking about it. And, even though she'd agreed they wouldn't do it again, her cheeks heated at the memory. 'No. No, we don't. I agree with you—we can't go back, Lewis. It's all done and gone.'

He nodded. 'And we don't want any awkwardness tipping over into our work, do we?'

Of course. This was just two people catching up after a long five years, trying to be normal. Trying to clear the air because they were colleagues. But here was the thing: Lewis never dealt with things like this head-on. He always shied away from conflict or difficult conversations but they were facing this awkward moment and he was totally in control. Maybe she wasn't the only one who'd changed, at least a little. 'No. No, we don't. I'd hate for anything to affect how we work together.'

'Okay, then. It's good that we agree.' He held up his glass, those soft, dark eyes capturing her gaze. God, he was so good to look at. He tipped his glass to hers. 'So…to friends and the future.'

'And flash-flooding forecasts.' She clinked his glass and laughed. 'Okay, tell me, what the heck have you been doing these last five years?'

'Not a lot, you know; just plodding along.'

He'd been promoted three times, apparently, but she wasn't surprised. He was damned good at his job.

He'd bought a house. Travelled to Laos, Cambodia and Singapore and had hiked in Australia. Been on three stag weekends and attended four of their mutual friends' weddings, which she'd decided not to come home for, because of so many reasons…mainly, Lewis.

He'd become an uncle to another girl, now three in total: Lola, Lily and Luna. Luna had been a surprise, but also a joy. Logan had said it was their last, but Lewis wasn't so sure. He'd spent yesterday afternoon at Lola's eighth birthday party, a tie-dye party, but he'd chosen not to wear his pink-and-orange T-shirt tonight. Then they'd cooked pizzas in Logan's outdoor pizza oven for the birthday tea.

All that, straight after the hotter than hot kiss.

How had he managed to function in public after that? She'd been a trembling wreck and had needed a lie down before being able to look her sister in the eye, while keeping the kiss a secret, close to her chest. Because why tell her something that might worry her, or excite her, when it had been a mistake?

She shook her head and tried to put thoughts of Lewis's mouth to the back of her mind. 'What is it with your family and names starting with L? I'm sure this wasn't a thing a few years ago.'

He laughed and shrugged. 'Don't ask me. Neither of our parents have L names, it's just something Logan's decided to do with his kids.'

'You obviously married the wrong sister, then. Should have been Lucy. She'd have fit right in.' She laughed, but stopped short when she saw his expression suddenly change from light to dark. His gaze dipped to his glass, then back to her. He paused a beat, then two.

She wished she could take it back but it was too late.

'I definitely married the right sister, Charlie.' He held her gaze and it felt simultaneously like a knife lancing her chest and her heart weakening. He'd thought he'd chosen well, but she'd left him. Would he have been better off with Lucy, with someone else? Would he have been happy?

She couldn't bear to think of him married to another woman, and yet, she'd been the one who'd filed for divorce. Torn apart by grief for her future, she'd wanted to make a positive move for a fresh start, for both of them. Perhaps if she'd stood on her own two feet from an earlier age, had made that stand for herself instead of letting everyone else take care of her, she might have been stronger at fighting for her marriage too.

She didn't know how to answer him, so scrambled around to change the subject. 'So, you bought a house? That's impressive, especially with house prices these days.'

'Yes.' Pride glittered in his eyes now. 'I finally

managed to get a mortgage. All grown-up, right? It's a do-up, but it's all mine. It's in Grey Lynn.'

All mine.

They'd been saving to buy their own house and had almost made enough for a deposit when everything had fallen apart. She shook herself and ignored the hurt slicing through her. They weren't going back that far, just covering the last five years. 'Oh! Lucy lives in Ponsonby. We must be almost neighbours.'

They shared address details; they were close but not quite neighbours.

'Walking distance, though. That's funny—I thought Lucy lived in Titirangi.' His eyebrows rose. 'It's weird, isn't it, that when a relationship breaks up you lose touch with people you were once close with?'

'I know. It's like a part of you is shirred off. I often wondered about Logan and your friends and, well…' *You.* Her throat felt scratchy—too much nostalgia. 'Anyway, after her split with Tony, Lucy moved to Grey Lynn.'

'They're not together any more? I didn't want to ask…you know…' He grimaced and shrugged again.

'Because *I'm* here looking after her, not him?'

'And because it's none of my business.'

It was once.

'Lucy wouldn't care if I told you; she's very open about it. Basically, he didn't want kids and bolted when Lucy fell pregnant.'

'What a guy.' He shook his head and took another drink of wine. There'd never been a big friendship between Lewis and Tony but they had met up at family gatherings. She tried not to think about the gaps that existed now, the empty places at the table whenever, if ever, the Rose family got together. Conversely, she'd also lost Lewis's twin brother and the cosy friendships they'd once all shared.

'Yes, well, Mum and Dad moved in with Lucy to help her for the first four weeks of Stella's life until Lucy pushed them to go to Uganda.'

Marcel arrived with the *amuse bouche*, which was a divine nibble of goat's cheese panna cotta and gone in one delicious mouthful. But she took the brief conversation hiatus to settle her emotions. Splitting with him had been the right decision at the time, so there was no point reliving the pain of getting used to life without him.

He looked up from his plate and smiled, much more relaxed than she was, especially now they'd agreed not to kiss again. 'What about you, Charlie? How have the five years been for you?'

'Oh. Work, mainly. Yes, work with a few weekend city breaks to places in Europe. I went to the Edinburgh Fringe a couple of times. Spent a fortnight in France. But, yeah, work… I couldn't afford to buy a flat in London on a single doctor's salary, so I rented. But that did make it easier for me to leave.'

'You enjoyed it over there?'

'Oh, yes. London is amazing. There's always something to do, new things popping up all the time. There's a real buzz—' She was interrupted by the drum of heavy rain on the window. It sounded like rapid gunfire: *rata-tata-rata*. Then it became louder and harder—hail now too. The cars in the street had slowed and somehow the night sky had got even darker. 'Looks like the flash-flooding forecast was right.'

'Got to love Auckland summer weather.' He shook his head, smiling. 'Do you think you'd ever have come home if it hadn't been for Lucy's illness?'

'Um…well… I have been back a couple of times, actually. Just briefly, for Christmas.' But she hadn't contacted him because she'd thought it would hurt too much, for herself and for him.

'Oh.' His eyes widened with a flash of disappointment. 'Yes, Christmas. Of course.'

'You don't think Mum and Dad would have let me get away with not being here for five years?'

'No. That is very true. Your parents would have hated not seeing you at Christmas.' He cleared his throat, not very good at hiding his emotion. Did he miss her at Christmas, on every birthday? Did he remember their anniversary and light a candle in memory of what they'd once had, the way she did?

He shook his head. 'Right. I wonder where that next course is?'

He turned and nodded at Marcel who came running over, took away their plates and poured them a small glass of Riesling to pair with their starter of prosciutto and pickles, accompanied by the most divine olive and rosemary focaccia she'd ever tasted.

Soon enough, Marcel was back with their fish course, then slow-roasted lamb plus a half-glass of Sangiovese, while she chatted with Lewis about the differences in hospital emergency rooms between London and Auckland, about baby girls, seeing as they had those in common, and about recent movies they'd seen.

They didn't talk about whether either of them had had any other relationships or about their feelings or their shared past. And, while it was a good catch-up, the shared past was glaringly the elephant in the room, there in every look and every word. Because they couldn't escape it, could they? But at some point they needed to face it, even if only to put it to rest.

They were both distracted momentarily by the blare of a car horn outside. The rain still hammered against the window, making them raise their voices to be heard.

'And now you're back.' He smiled and she thought he might actually be okay with her being here. At least, now they'd had this chance to talk.

She found herself smiling too. Who would have thought she'd be sitting here doing this with Lewis? 'Yes, I'm back.'

He turned his warm gaze back to her. 'In a high-level job you must have worked hard to get. Well done. You always were a high flyer.'

'Thanks.' He'd always been her cheerleader, and she'd always let him be. Until the end, when she'd realised he was using his support of her to abnegate his own emotional needs. 'Well, I had to negotiate hard for the part-time bit, but I've promised to increase my hours once Lucy feels better. I'm not that desperate mess I was back then; I can manage full time just fine under normal circumstances. I just want to be able to give Stella and Lucy my time and attention.'

Um...like you are right now?

She pushed away her guilt at leaving them at home. Lucy had all but shoved her out of the door anyway.

'You were never a mess, Charlie, just messed up by grief and disappointment. There's a difference.' He paused for a beat, his eyes roving over her face, her mouth. 'I hope I've changed too. I'd have done things differently.'

What did he mean? 'You would...?'

Her words were stolen by another blare of a horn, so long and so loud, they could hear it from their table.

CHAPTER SEVEN

'WHAT THE HELL? Did you hear that?' Lewis tore his eyes away from Charlie's exquisite features and tried to listen to the street noises, trying to zone out the restaurant chatter.

The horn sounded again, then there was shouting.

He glanced at Charlie and she nodded, clearly reading his mind. Something bad had happened and they were duty-bound, and *needed*, to go and help. He jumped up and rushed to the door, pausing only for a moment to hold it open for her.

'Over there!' He pointed to a small crowd at the other side of the road. The traffic had come to a standstill so they quickly jogged across.

'Excuse me. 'Scuse me. I'm a paramedic and Charlie is a doctor. Can someone tell us what's happened?' He gently squeezed through the huddle of strangers to find a young woman, soaked through with rain, kneeling in the road and talking to an elderly gentleman, who was lying on the ground, pale, shocked and obviously in pain.

The young woman looked up at him and blinked through the rain. 'This is Graham. He was running across the road, trying to dodge the traffic, and suddenly collapsed. I don't know if he tripped or what, but he hit the ground with a real bump. And now he tells me he's got back and arm pain.'

'Okay, thanks.' Charlie turned to the crowd as Lewis knelt to assess the man. Had it been a trip or a collapse? 'Has anyone called an ambulance?'

The woman nodded. 'Yes, I did.'

'Great, thank you. We've got this now.'

'Brilliant.' She turned to Graham. 'Graham? Graham, this is a paramedic. He's going to help you.'

'And, lucky for us all, we've a doctor here too,' Lewis said to Graham as Charlie knelt in a puddle to start her examination. He turned to the crowd as he stripped off his jacket and laid it over the man in an attempt to keep him warm.

'Can someone ask in the restaurants for a blanket? We need to keep our friend here as warm and dry as possible. And can someone please redirect the traffic? Otherwise we'll be snarled up from here to Hamilton. You…perfect.' He pointed to a guy who was filming everything on his mobile phone; best to keep him occupied with something else. 'Please put that away. I'm sure our friend here doesn't want this all over the Internet. And can someone else please keep an eye out for the ambulance and direct them here? Right…' He turned back to Charlie. 'How are we doing?'

'Graham's got a blinding headache, but is managing to tell me where else he's got pain. He's trying not to move and I think that's a very good idea.' She looked up at Lewis and nodded, water dripping off her nose, and she blinked more rain out of her eyes. But she focused and he read between the lines. Graham had a possible head and neck injury but was conscious and responsive, all of which were good signs. 'Pain in his right wrist. Swelling and accompanying grazes on his elbow, palm and forehead. What was that…?' She looked back at their patient. 'What's that? Chest pain.'

He watched her fingers go instinctively to Graham's radial pulse point. She looked up warily. 'Thready. Weak. Irregular.'

Not good. Did he have a history of heart problems? 'Anyone here with Graham?' Lewis asked the now-diminishing crowd.

No one answered. The poor guy was on his own. And that meant there was no information.

'Graham? Graham, can you hear me? Damn. Graham?' Charlie's voice grew louder. 'Graham.' She put her hands to the man's carotid artery and shook her head. Then she put her face close to the man's lips and shook her head again. 'Lewis, cardiac arrest…'

After checking his airway, she tipped Graham's head back, lifted his chin, pinched his nose and put her mouth over his, then blew twice.

Lewis watched for Graham's chest to rise and fall with Charlie's breaths then he knelt alongside

Graham, placed the heel of his hand over the centre of the man's chest and started compressions, counting quickly. 'One, two, three…'

'Hey! Can you go look for an AED…defibrillator…please?' Charlie called to a passer-by. 'Ask in a shop. The museum. Any public space.'

'Twenty-nine, thirty…' Lewis called and she blew again twice.

Lewis nodded and started compressions again. 'One, two, three…'

'Where's that ambulance?' Charlie stood and peered down the car-blocked road. 'Can someone please provide some privacy? Stand here and here…' She directed three people, totally in command. But then, this was her turf.

And it was his. He huffed out, 'Twenty-nine, thirty.'

He leant back as she did mouth-to-mouth again. 'I can hear a distant siren but it's probably stuck in this snarled traffic.'

'Then we don't give up.'

'We don't give up.' Lewis nodded as he took her in. Her face was set and determined, her tone positive but guarded. Her hair was stuck to her cheeks, her clothes completely saturated. But her eyes blazed with a resolve bordering on stubbornness. She would not give up.

And she was quite possibly the most beautiful he'd ever seen her.

They did not give up. Not when the crowd began

to disperse. Not when the hail started again, hitting them like pellets of ice on their faces and hands. Not when the paramedics finally arrived—Emma and Raj, Lewis's colleagues. Not until Graham had pads attached to his chest and had been shocked twice then bundled into the ambulance and taken away.

Lewis watched the ambulance drive away, wishing he could be in there, giving the drugs and doing the hard yards to keep Graham alive. But he was also glad he was here, with Charlie, sharing this most profound experience.

She was talking to someone in the crowd, thanking them for their help. As she said goodbye, she turned, caught his eye and walked over to him, the friendly smile she'd put on for the bystander slipping to reveal her real thoughts. She inhaled deeply then blew out slowly. 'We did our best, right?'

He grimaced. 'We did.'

They both knew the odds of Graham being alive when he arrived at the emergency department were slim to none. And, even though they lived and breathed this kind of scenario every day, and had both learnt to deal with loss and the fragile human condition, he wanted to put his arms round her and hold her close. Because this was different. This was them against the odds and the elements.

It seemed they could work in perfect harmony even if they couldn't live in it.

Couldn't: past tense. Could never again, he reminded himself. Their chance was over. They were different people now, and still bruised from what had happened before. It would be madness to try get any of it back.

We don't give up.

You stay.

But they had given up on themselves. They'd stopped talking, stopped kissing, stopped being *them*. They'd become disparate people living under the same roof.

He'd stayed. But staying hadn't helped, had it? He'd thrown all his energy into making her feel better and had ignored his own needs. He'd pushed them aside and refused to talk about how he felt.

And it had all been for nothing, because how could she have stayed with someone who'd refused to acknowledge there was a problem, especially when the problem ended up being him?

He should have been open to talking about adoption or surrogacy, but he hadn't been able to see past her pain, and had thought talking about alternatives to her carrying a child would be even more painful.

God, he didn't know, even now, whether she'd thought about those options since, once the rawness had faded. Maybe in time, if they'd stuck it out, they'd have reached a place where they could have talked about that. The thought made his heart ache. So many missed opportunities because they'd been enmeshed in so much grief.

She shook her head and then her arms, and laughed as water sprayed and sluiced onto the ground. 'Ugh. I am completely soaked.'

'So I see.' He laughed and his gaze grazed her wet top which showed the outline of her bra.

Lace...

Something deep inside him flared. *Stop.* But how could he help it? She was freaking beautiful. Not just because she looked amazing, all dishevelled and undone, but because she didn't care about getting wet and cold for the sake of someone who needed her skills.

'Ah.' She tugged her jacket around her breasts and then put her palm on his chest. Even though they were both cold, her touch was warm and steady, unlike his heart. 'You didn't even have a jacket on. Wow, your heart is beating very fast, Lewis.'

'Cardiac compressions can do that to a guy.' As could the tender touch of a beautiful woman. And the thought of what was beneath her lacy bra.

'Mr Parry!' It was Marcel calling from across the road, outside the restaurant. He ducked between the now slow-moving cars making his way towards them. 'Thought you might be still here.'

Lewis glanced at the restaurant. The closed sign hung in the window. 'Hi. Yes, sorry we had to dash off like that. There was a medical emergency and we had to help.'

'Not a problem. How is he?'

Lewis sighed. 'Touch and go, to be honest.'

'Well, thank you for being there for him, especially on a night like this.' Marcel held up a brown paper carrier bag. 'You missed your dessert but I've packed it up for you. Plus some sticky wine to go with it.'

'Sticky?' Charlie frowned. He could feel her shivering next to him.

The restaurant owner laughed. 'Dessert wine— thick and sweet and delicious. You'll like it.'

'You know, I've never tried dessert wine.' Charlie beamed at Marcel. 'Thank you.'

'Yes, thank you, Marcel. That's very kind.' Lewis took the paper bag and thought if it got any more soggy it might not last the trip back to the hotel, only a couple of streets away.

Once Marcel had returned to his restaurant, Charlie looked at her phone. 'I'm freezing. I'm going to call a cab and go home.'

No. Lewis's gut contracted. He wasn't ready to let her go, because they hadn't really talked, had they? They'd only just started to unpack things before Graham's emergency had interrupted everything. But they were both soaked and cold. It was probably a good idea to end the night now, before he read too much into the warmth of her palm on his chest and the way she sometimes looked at him with regret, sadness and...desire. 'Sounds good.'

But a frown formed as she looked at the car-hire app, her teeth chattering now. 'Is there something else going on tonight—a gig or big sports game? Because I can't seem to get any take-up on my ride home. *Oh*... It's not even responding now. I've just got the swirl of doom on my screen. Maybe the app's down, or my phone's drowned.'

'I'll give it a go.' He pulled out his phone, trying to keep his own shivering under control. 'Nope, nothing. Look, my hotel is literally two streets away. Why don't you come up to my room, dry off and wait until the app's working again? Or wait until the alcohol's worn off enough for me to be safe to drive you.'

'Go to your hotel?' Her gaze tangled with his and, despite the shivering and teeth chattering, her eyes misted the way they'd always used to when she'd been all turned on. 'I... I don't know, Lewis.'

But he knew it wasn't just a question of whether they should go together, it was a question of what might happen. Because the warmth of her palm was good. The desire in her eyes was better.

The flare of need inside him threatened to overwhelm him. But they'd agreed, nothing was going to happen.

Nothing could happen.

CHAPTER EIGHT

GO TO HIS HOTEL?

Charlotte's head filled with all the things that could happen in a hotel room with Lewis. They had form, right? Back when they'd been married, a hotel room had always meant sex. They had a relationship history of many hotel rooms and lots of good times. History that should not be repeated.

And yet, that kiss yesterday had been…hot. And needed, and like some kind of switch that had flipped her world upside down. Because she couldn't deny that she wanted to do it again…and again…and again. So going to his hotel would be dangerous. 'I… I don't know, Lewis.'

He blinked as rain ran in rivulets down his cheeks, then he pulled her into a doorway out of the rain. 'Because what? You think I'll make a move? No way, Charlie. We agreed, right?'

'Yes, we agreed.' Although, up close with him in a doorway, she was currently regretting that agreement.

Stop it.

His eyes widened. 'So, where's the harm? We are both completely soaked and shivering. That is not good. What if you're waiting for half an hour for a cab? I don't want you getting hypothermia on my watch.'

The harm was, she didn't think she could keep her promise if she was in a hotel room with him. But she *was* freezing and completely drenched and he was holding up the soggy restaurant takeaway bag saying, 'There's pudding too.'

And she'd always been a sucker for dessert. 'Oh, okay. Just until I'm dry and warm.'

'Come on, then.' He stretched out his hand and she grabbed it and ran with him through the Auckland streets to his hotel. She was holding Lewis's hand. And it felt so instinctively right and good.

But when they entered the hotel and he had to retrieve his room key from his wallet, he let go, pausing for a moment as he looked at her, then at their hands. 'Sorry. Habit, I guess.'

'It's okay. It helped us get here quicker, that's all. I'm not sure I'd have kept up with you otherwise. You're very fit, Lewis.'

'I try.' He grinned and she followed him into the lift, her heart sagging, but knowing he was right. Kissing and hand-holding were not on the agenda. The question she had to ask herself, then, was… what was really on the agenda here? Because she could have waited for a cab, or even got a bus. She could have taken her share of the dessert home and given half to Lucy.

But all questions were forgotten when she

walked into the penthouse suite he'd been given. The walls were dark slatted wood, the furnishings made of the softest cream leather and the curtains were a lovely, soft taupe linen. It was all very top-end and luxurious. 'Wow. This is seriously expensive and very, very swanky. I bet it's a great view on a fine day.'

'When I checked in this afternoon, I could see right out over the harbour bridge and up to the North Shore,' he said. But all they could see now was the rain lashing against the floor-to-ceiling windows. 'It's also got an outside fire pit, but that's a bit redundant tonight. Go hop in the shower; I'll plate this up. You want a hot drink too?' He pulled out a drawer in a console. 'There's a kettle and coffee and tea here.'

She was so cold, her body had gone from shivering to bone-rattling and her fingers were numb. 'Can you see if they've got hot chocolate?'

He grinned and his eyes grew wide and wicked. 'Hot chocolate, dessert wine *and* pudding—now you're talking. I'll see what I can do. Go—shower.'

The shower was glorious, with high-end shower gel, shampoo and conditioner and a rain showerhead. *This* rain was going to be hot and healing. Although she probably should have a cold shower if she was going to get through dessert with Lewis.

She scrubbed and shampooed herself and then wrapped her hair in a thick towel and drew a fluffy white robe round her naked body. When she went back into the bedroom, she found him standing by the console, stirring a cup of something that smelt delicious. He'd changed out of his wet clothes and was now in a dry pair of shorts and T-shirt. He glanced up as she approached, his eyes warm and soft as he smiled. 'Feel better?'

That smile was so good, it made her insides tingle. 'Oh, yes. I've stopped shivering, and these towels are *so* fluffy. Your turn.'

He shook his head. 'It's okay. I'll just finish making the hot drinks.'

'Lewis, please. You must be freezing.'

'No. You…' He looked as if he was about to say something more but closed his mouth. 'As it happens, I am cold, actually. Can you finish off stirring these? I won't be long.'

You…what? Had he been about to put her needs above his again? But he hadn't, had he? He'd stopped himself. *Interesting.* It was a small thing, but the second time she'd noticed he'd put his needs first. That was good; he needed to do that.

She could hear him singing in the bathroom like he used to at home. Always the same tune, Rihanna's *Umbrella.* Which was pretty appropriate right now.

But…*home.* Her gut tightened in sadness. They'd loved that little rented cottage in Parnell. they'd made it theirs with the pieces of furniture they'd carefully chosen from second-hand shops.

It had been hard leaving that place too, hard leaving him.

She heard the water running and imagined him in there, and wondered how the last five years had changed his body. She'd met him at high school and had watched with delight as he'd grown from lanky, sporty teenager to a man. She'd encouraged him to follow his dream of being a paramedic and celebrated when he got accepted on the course and when he'd graduated top of the class.

He'd kept himself fit for his job by running, swimming and gym work. She'd always loved the hard ridges of his muscles, the way she'd felt so safe and wanted in his arms. The way he'd looked at her as they'd made love.

She recalled the words he'd whispered to her on their wedding night: *I promise I'll always love you, Charlie. Whatever happens. I don't want a life without you. Ever.*

But, even so, she'd forced him to have one. Tears threatened, prickling the back of her eyes. Her heart hurt.

God, Lewis...

The door lock clicked and she swallowed back her regret and sadness. She must not show him how she felt. Which was...what exactly? Mixed up. *Turned on.* More... All the feelings, all the things.

Was she just hankering for what they'd once had? She didn't know. But something new beat inside her and she couldn't ignore it. She also didn't know what the hell to do with it, because it seemed to be beating louder and harder every second she spent with him.

He came out of the bathroom in a cloud of steam, dressed again in his shorts and T shirt and, disappointingly, not just with a small towel at his waist.

Had she really been hoping for that?

Yes, she had. She'd been secretly hoping to see him half-naked.

All naked, actually.

Oh, God, she had it bad. Why hadn't she stayed, tried harder?

She settled on the comfortable chair next to the little coffee table in the middle of the room, tucked her feet up under her bottom and cradled her mug, relishing the scent and taking little sips just for something to take her focus away from Lewis. 'This is delicious.'

'Excellent.' He grabbed his cup and drank, leaning against the console. His eyes widened. 'Wow. It really is. Everything in here is next level.'

'I wanted to say, you did good before, Lewis—with the CPR. In all our years together, I never actually saw you working. You're very professional. Amazing.'

'That's high praise from an emergency doctor; thanks. You too.' He rubbed his hair dry with a hand towel. 'It wasn't easy kneeling on wet tarmac trying to save someone's life. But you didn't hesitate.'

'Of course not. And neither did you. But I think I've got gravel burns on my knees.' She examined them: just a little bruising. She looked up and caught him looking at her legs too. 'Do you still love your job?'

'Absolutely. There is nothing I'd rather do for work.' His gaze moved to her face. 'You? Emergency medicine was always on your radar. Are you glad you chose it?'

'Hell, yes. I love the urgency and the adrenalin rush. And I love helping people.'

'You always did.' He thought for a moment. 'I wonder how Graham's doing.'

'I don't have great hopes, I'm afraid.'

Lewis's eyebrows rose as he sat down opposite her. 'I'll ask at work tomorrow.'

'Or I could.' She bugged her eyes at him and chuckled.

He laughed and scrubbed a hand through his tousled hair. 'This is so weird. Who would have thought I'd be working with you? And be *here* in a hotel room with you?'

She glanced down at her towelling robe. Half-naked in a hotel room; once upon a time, he'd have slipped his hands in between the robe folds and made some sexy comment.

She tightened the tie at her waist. 'Well, who else would you like to be in a hotel room with?

Please don't tell me you still have a crush on Amanda Seyfried?'

'Oh, *Mamma Mia*.' He made a 'chef's kiss' gesture, bringing his thumb and two fingers to his mouth and flaring them out. 'There's just something about her I can't let go of. She was in the best movies of my youth.'

'Um…you were late teens when *Mamma Mia* came out.' She laughed. She'd always ribbed him about his love for the actress who'd played the starring role in the movie. She knew him so well—*had* known him so well—and suddenly she wanted to fill the important gaps in her knowledge of him, even though some of his answers might hurt her. 'Have you…um…dated anyone since… you know…? Is it okay to ask?'

'Sure.' He blinked, obviously a little taken aback. 'I guess we were bound to get round to this conversation at some point. I've been out with a couple of women, yes.'

Why had she asked him that when any answer other than *no* would stab her heart? 'Oh? And…?'

He shrugged and sat back. 'Didn't work out. You?'

'A couple of dinner dates, nothing more. When I got to London I decided to throw myself into my job. Seemed a lot easier than getting into another relationship.'

'So nothing serious?' He drained his hot chocolate, his expression one that said, 'seriously, you haven't had sex for five years?'

'Nothing much at all. It took a long time to come to terms with everything. I didn't feel I had a lot to offer someone.'

He put his cup down and frowned at her. 'Please, Charlie. For God's sake. You've got so much to offer anyone.'

'Oh, I'm not saying it to get sympathy. Just, most guys our age are looking to settle down and I couldn't commit to anything. Not after…you.'

He inhaled sharply, took a moment, then leaned forward and touched her hand. 'Charlie, I'm sorry I broke it. I didn't give you what you needed. I thought I was saying and doing the right things but in hindsight…' His voice trailed off but he kept on looking at her. Kept his hand on hers.

'Hell, even I didn't know what I needed, so don't beat yourself up about that.' She shook her head. So here they were, suddenly in the thick of it. There was so much they needed to unpack, and yet at the same time she wondered if they should venture into their past at all. Because it might only drum up the old arguments and they'd be no further on, except five years older. '*I* left, Lewis. I broke it. Me and my stupid uterus.'

'Don't ever say that. Nothing about you is stupid, Charlie. Nothing at all.' His jaw set as he looked at her. And in his expression she saw so many tangled emotions that mirrored hers: confusion, desire, affection. Fear…yes, fear, because they were treading new territory here. Forging something out of the ashes of their marriage…. *friendship?*

Everything was loaded with the weight of their break-up and there needed to be some honesty before anything, including their fledging friendship, could grow. And here tonight, after they'd shared something so momentous as trying to save a life, it felt right to do a deep dive.

She rested her cup on her knee and tried to explain her version of what had happened after she'd left. 'I had some counselling, you know. Talked myself silly going round and round. But eventually I came to terms with why I was so devastated by it all.'

She didn't know why she'd suddenly blurted out that particular thing but it felt right to say something, to show him and herself that she'd tried to understand everything.

He frowned. 'Because the infertility was a shock. Because it was cruel, Charlie.'

'Yes.' *The* infertility—not *your* infertility. Lewis generally chose his words carefully. Maybe he still didn't see it as just *her* problem. She didn't know how to feel about that. 'And because I felt as if I let everyone down.'

'Whoa. No way.' He raised his palm. 'That wasn't it at all. I didn't feel let down. I hurt for you—with you.'

'I know, but I could see in your eyes how you pretended you were okay about it but, deep down, you weren't. You couldn't have been okay with it. You had this idea of what a perfect family looked like...'

'Sure. I always wanted a family, you know that. Especially after my crappy childhood, being shunted from pillar to post because my mum didn't actually want or like children, and my dad never, ever being in the picture. I missed not having a dad like other kids. I missed my mum a lot too.'

He hauled in a breath. 'In my head, I had this blueprint of a family: two kids, two parents; probably something I'd seen on TV. But if I ever did it I wanted to get it right. I wanted to have what Logan and I never had, what Logan is creating with Alice and the girls. Is that such a bad thing— to want to love your own child? To have a tight bond? To be *present*?'

'Not at all. You deserve to have that, Lewis.' She took a breath, her chest constricting. 'But when I couldn't do that you still said everything would be okay, everything was fine. It was like you weren't listening or understanding the situation.' She watched his expression, hoping she wasn't hurting him all over again. Because they were actually talking about this—really *talking*— for the first time.

But he just smiled sadly. 'I wanted you to believe in yourself the way I believed in you.'

Her heart squeezed. 'And I just felt trapped by impossible dreams I couldn't fulfil.'

His expression hollowed out to one of shock and uncertainty. '*Trapped* by me?'

She drew her gaze away from him, swallowing down the raw lump in her throat. 'By you, by my parents, by other people's expectations: to carry on the family doctoring tradition; bear the grandchildren my parents desperately wanted; provide the family you so desperately deserved to have. Your mother wasn't there for you when you grew up, Lewis. You scratched a family out of distant relatives. You and Logan clung to each other and you both deserved to grow something good for yourselves. Logan has done that; you need that too. But I couldn't…can't…do that for you. And no amount of you telling me everything was going to be fine was going to magically make things what they weren't.'

He swallowed as he digested her words. 'You were struggling; I was trying to make it better for you.'

'I know. And you did. *You did.*' She ached to soothe away the hurt they'd both endured during that rocky time. 'But rightly or wrongly I felt as if there was a sheen of facade, a brave face rather than an honest one. You never told me how you *felt* about it all. It was like trying to talk to a rock.'

'I was trying to *be* a rock for you—staunch and solid. If I said it was all okay, it would be. If

I said we'd get through it, we would. I was trying to be a support. Have you any idea how hard it is to see someone you love cry every day for eighteen months? To endure endless painful tests and investigations? And to have nothing...*nothing...* you can do to help them? To see them closed off, hibernating under the duvet, refusing to come out, to *live*? Then to see the anger rip through them, to come home to broken plates and slashed cushions? To not know which Charlotte I was actually coming home to? Depressed Charlotte, angry Charlotte, numb Charlotte...'

He shook his head, eyes sad. 'I tried; God help me I did. I knew you were hurting so badly but I didn't know what else to do, other than try make you believe things would be okay.'

Her lips trembled and she pressed them together. Because she had been that person—she wasn't now, but she had been. Torn apart by despair, she'd allowed her emotions to engulf her. 'I was devastated and I took it out on you. But I could see you were broken too. You just wanted to hide that from me.'

His dark-brown eyes blazed then. 'Damn right I did. I was protecting you. I didn't want to make you feel worse by adding my feelings to the mix.'

'And that...right there. That's why I had to go, Lewis. We'd always talked openly about having kids. You were thrilled when Logan had his. You were, and I'm sure still are, an amazing uncle.

But, when it came to us, you couldn't admit how disappointed you were. You clammed up. You refused to talk about your feelings.

'But I saw it. I tried to get through to you. I pushed you because I didn't want you to resent me further down the track. But the more I pushed, the more distant you became. Then I got angry…with you and the unfairness of having our plans taken away. And then I stopped trying. In the end, it felt like were living separate lives. We both deserved more than that.'

He shook his head, his eyes flickering closed for a beat. When he looked up at her again, he saw fathomless sadness there. 'I'm so sorry. I thought saying that everything would be okay was what you wanted to hear. And I realise I was wrong; I see that now. I've thought about it so much over the years and I get it. But back then I loved you so much, Charlie. I just wanted you to stop hurting.'

Loved: past tense. But, hell, what else could she expect? That he'd held a torch for her these last few years? That he'd put his life on hold until she decided to come back? No. But the loss of it reverberated through her, core-deep.

She reached out and stroked her fingertips across his jaw, because this was so profound, so damned deep, she couldn't sit there and not touch him. She needed to feel the physical connection as well as the emotional one. 'You know what? I don't even know what I wanted to hear back then except for, *I'm sorry, Mrs Parry, we made a mistake. Of course you can have a baby.'*

'I wish that had happened, Charlie. I really do. More than anything.' His eyes glistened. 'And I'm sorry I got it so wrong.'

She moved her hand from his cheek and knitted her fingers with his. 'Oh, we were so young, Lewis. And blindsided at the news. I'd always had everything given to me on a plate. I had you, my doting parents and a loving sister, and you all conspired to keep me happy and boost my ego and soothe my journey through life. God knows why.'

'Because we loved you, Charlie. Plain and simple.'

Loved: there it was again. 'And I'd had it so easy up until then. I'd never failed at anything before and didn't know how to cope with it all.'

'And I refused to discuss some things. I refused to acknowledge how I felt.'

'Which was?' She waited, wondering if he had enough personal growth and faith in her to be honest. 'How did you feel about what *you'd* lost?'

'You want me to say those things? That I was broken up that I couldn't be a dad? That it hurt whenever I saw pregnant women, or when I held little Lola? It hurt that I'd never have that; I'd never get to watch my son play football.'

'Or do ballet?' She smiled, because it was never going to happen for her, but if it did for Lewis…if someone was lucky enough to find him and keep him…then he needed to be open to all opportunities for his kids.

'Or ballet. I didn't say those things because I didn't want you to hurt more.' He exhaled a long breath, then looked her full in the eyes. He hesitated and closed his eyes briefly. When he opened them, he nodded sadly. 'I was gutted, if I'm honest. Absolutely broken.'

Finally.

She let go of the breath she felt she'd been holding for nearly six and a half years, since that day at the doctor when they'd got the terrible news. Finally, he was being honest. *Finally.* She felt hollowed out, as broken as he was describing, but also felt relief too. This was a breakthrough for them.

Tears sprang in her eyes and she fisted them away. 'I'm sorry, Lewis. So sorry we couldn't fulfil your dream. But thank you for telling me the truth.'

'I should have done it a long time ago.'

The dream hadn't fallen apart because of her uterus. The dream had fallen apart because they'd been unable to deal with that. 'Were we too young? Was that it? Too disconnected from each other or too immature to deal with such big personal issues?'

Her parents had never wanted them to get married so young. It had almost been a case of 'told you so' when she'd left him. *You should have listened to us; we know what's best for you.*

'We did the best we could at the time. Two hurting people who didn't know what to do.' He brought her hand to his mouth, kissing it gently, the way he used to back when things between them had been a whole lot better. She shivered at the touch of his lips on her skin. There was something so intimate in such a small gesture, it almost overpowered her.

She needed some space before she crawled into his lap and kissed him properly again, long and hard. She took a deep breath, then another, trying to find her equilibrium again. She slipped her hand from his, found a smile and made it real... for Lewis. 'Hey, you know what's going to make us both feel better?'

'I'm all ears.' He smiled, the glistening eyes dry now.

'Marcel's pudding. And what about that wine? It would be a shame not to have it.'

You were supposed to be leaving, Charlie.

But she needed some light relief before going home and facing Lucy's questions.

One little taste...*of the wine.*

'Excellent idea, Dr Rose.' He looked relieved to be chartering less difficult territory as he jumped up to find plates, arrange the dessert items on a large one and then pull a piece of card out of the bag. 'There's a copy of the menu here. Looks like these are mini almond-and-espresso cannoli, and chocolate-and-salted-caramel bom…boloni… bomboloni.' He stumbled over the Italian word, then brought the plate to the little coffee table. 'That must be these little doughnut-shaped things. And…mini cheesecake.'

'Oh, *yes!*' Charlie fist-pumped the air. 'I'm going to go for the chee—'

'Cheesecake first? Your favourite, right?' He laughed and handed her a glass of the wine he'd just opened. 'Try it with some of this.'

There was a new ease to the atmosphere now— breathing space, an understanding. Things felt brighter inside her, as if the weight of nearly seven years…the difficult last two of their marriage and five apart…was lifting.

She bit into the cheesecake, which was light and yet rich, followed by a mouthful of the wine. 'Oh, okay, it's sweet, all right. Oh. Wow.' She blinked and swallowed. 'Okay. There's a lot going on there. That's…different.'

He grinned. 'Yes, but what do you think?'

'It's like drinking jam. Winey jam. Jammy wine.' She laughed. 'Is it strong?'

He examined the bottle. 'Only fourteen and a half percent.'

'Hmm. Strong enough.' She had another mouthful. 'Okay, I'm getting used to it. It's nice— yummy, actually.

'Let me try again then, ahem: flash-flooding

forecast. Flash flooding florecast.' She giggled. 'Imagine me after more than one glass.'

'Lightweight.' He leaned forward across the little table to pick up a mini cannoli at the same time she did. Their noses almost touched. He inhaled sharply as he captured her gaze. *'God.'*

'What?' Her forehead brushed against his. He smelt of expensive shampoo. He smelt good. She was acutely aware of him so close, so here, so… Lewis.

'Your laugh. Your smile…' He ran the back of his fingertips down her cheek. 'Jeez, Charlie.'

She closed her eyes and tried to swallow away the rush of desire but found herself curling towards his fingers and his heat.

'Lewis,' she whispered, every cell in her body straining for his touch.

No. They'd agreed. But he was so damned irresistible.

She drew away, picked up a *bombol…* doughnutty thing…and held it to his mouth. He took a bite and sighed. 'Oh, my God. You have got to try this.' He took the leftover half from her fingers and held it to her lips. 'Try it, Charlie. Bomboloni is "the bomb". This is the best thing you'll taste all night.'

I hope not.

She opened her mouth and bit into the bomboloni. Salted caramel and chocolate cream burst onto her tongue, sweet, salty and delicious. 'Oh, God, that is heaven.'

He edged away slightly and looked at her, cupping her cheek with his palm. 'No, darling. You are.'

The world stopped turning right then and shrank to that room, that night, that man. She swallowed then cleared her throat. 'But, Lewis… We said…' She didn't have the fight in her to say any more. She wanted it—wanted him.

He shrugged. 'Hey, I'm trying here, I promise. But you are so damned gorgeous. I tried to not be attracted to you. I tried not to notice how amazing you looked when you arrived at the restaurant. I tried not to look at your gorgeous nipples through your wet top. I'm trying to be platonic but I'm failing…badly.'

She gasped at his words, her body tingling with the rush of need rippling through her, and laughed as she remembered her restaurant entrance: dripping wet with a useless umbrella held over her soggy hair. 'I was drenched.'

'You looked beautiful to me.'

She curled her fingers round his wrist. His pulse beat fast and furious against her fingers. 'Please, Lewis. Don't try bolster me up. I know I looked a mess.'

'I'm telling you the truth, Charlie. I like you all undone.' His eyes flickered closed briefly, as if he was wrestling with his self-control. Clearly he failed, as he whispered, 'I particularly like the way you're looking at me right now.'

She swallowed, her grip on her own self-control weakening with every word he said. 'Like how?'

'Like you want to kiss me.'

CHAPTER NINE

HE DIDN'T WAIT for her answer. He knew his Charlie—knew when she was turned on, knew how to make her so. Knew when she needed to be kissed, and right now she needed it as much as he did.

He stood up and strode towards her, framing her cheek with his palm as he bent and slid his lips over hers. She gripped his shoulder and moaned, whispering his name like a sacred psalm. 'Lewis. Lewis. *Lewis...*'

She closed her eyes and sank into the kiss, sliding her tongue into his mouth and deepening their connection even more.

His pulse sky-rocketed. Need heated him. *She* heated him. This evening had been so intense, the embers of what they'd once had crashing back into full, incandescent life. The raw honesty was something only they could share. No one else had experienced the things they'd been through, and there was a new and deeper connection, so much swelling emotion between them—he and his amazing wife.

Ex-wife... The thought fleetingly assailed him and threatened to douse the desire coursing through him. But he pushed away all the pain and hurt from the past. She was here, she wanted him and, right now, he wanted this new version of her. She was sexier, more beautiful, more fun than he remembered and the way she was looking at him stoked the fire prickling over his skin, under his skin and deep in his belly.

There was only one way this could go. The kiss started soft and slow, achingly familiar and yet different too. He felt a new, heightened thrum of desire between them, the frank honesty lacing their connection and tightening it. He'd never wanted a woman as damned much as he did right now.

She tasted of jammy wine and chocolate; of the past and the now—this moment, this woman. *Charlie.* The first woman he'd ever loved. The only woman he'd ever loved.

He needed to explore her, to feel her tight against him, so he broke the kiss and offered his hand. She took it, standing up and stroking her palm across his chest. He kissed the top of her head, her forehead, her nose. He imprinted the new things he noticed into his memory banks: the scent of high-end shower gel; little laughter lines at the corners of her eyes. 'I can't get enough of you, Charlie. Stay the night?'

Her teeth worried at her bottom lip as she stared up at him, those beautiful blue eyes glittering with need but also concern. 'Lucy… She might be worried.'

Not a refusal, just hesitation.

'Call her, then—see if she's okay. Then stay.' His lips were on her throat and he murmured the words against her skin. 'I want you so much. I need this, Charlie, and I think you do too.'

'I do. But…' She kissed him again, long and slow. Then she pulled away, picked up her bag from the floor and rummaged for her phone. 'Hang on a second.'

She wrote a text and showed it to him, smiling, before sending it.

Luce, hey. Just checking in. Got stuck in rain downpour and now drying off at Lewis's hotel. Car hire apps are down. Might not be back until morning.

'Excellent. Might as well keep busy while we wait for her reply.' He tipped her chin so he could kiss her again. This time it was a slow burn kiss, backlit with a lightning show from the midnight sky. They were literally on top of the world, the forces of nature outside amplifying the potency of their passion in the penthouse.

Her hands slid down his back and pulled him tightly against her. She pressed against him and, when he slid his leg between hers, she moaned and rubbed her core against it. Her eyes flashed pure sex as she looked at him. 'God, Lewis, I want you so much.'

'You drive me crazy.' His body flooded with a deep, long-forgotten hunger as he slid his hand into the folds of her robe, finding her nipple and stroking until the tight bud peaked. Then he cupped her breast, relishing the soft silk of her skin and the misting of her eyes as he stroked and caressed.

Her phone beeped.

'Damn.' She reached for it, tutted then giggled. Then she showed him her sister's response:

You should change professions, sis. Novelist would be good. Fiction is your strong suit. You could just have told me you were having sex. Lucky thing. I would say be careful but you're a grown adult and you never listen to me anyway. See you in the morning. Have a good night.

He guffawed. 'Your sister has the measure of you.'

'Of you, more like.' She shook her head.

'Me? How? I'm just looking after you until the car hire app works.' He made to look all innocent, when he actually felt the complete opposite: desperate for her; carnal, base.

'Sure you are. Come here.' Laughing, she tugged at the neck of his T-shirt and brought him closer. Her hands were trembling.

He stilled and tilted her chin, looking deep into her eyes. 'You're shaking. Are you sure about this, Charlie?'

'I'm more sure about this than anything ever in my life.' She frowned. 'You have to ask?'

'Yes, I do. This…it's a lot.'

'It is. And I don't know what it means. I just know that I want it now. I want *you* now. Tonight.' She kissed his throat. 'I have no idea what it'll mean tomorrow, though.'

'That we're two grown adults who make rash decisions based on intense sexual craving and a deep sense of nostalgia, fuelled by adrenalin from a recent intense CPR situation?' Laughing, he slid his hand down to her thigh and whispered, 'Basically, I want to be deep inside you, Charlie. And damned quickly.'

'You've got such a way with words.' She giggled then put her arms round his neck and kissed his throat. 'Intense sexual craving…huh? I like the sound of that. Now, where were we?'

'I think…we were about here…' Her towelling robe had slipped down one shoulder, revealing her breast, and he slid his hand across the naked nipple and watched desire and delight heat her face. But when he looked back at her body he was jolted by the yellow-black bruising across her shoulder. He shuddered. 'I hate to see you so bruised, Charlie. I don't want to hurt you. Tell me to stop any time.'

'I'm not made of paper, Lewis. I'm a tough old cookie these days.' She kissed his jaw, then his mouth. By the time she pulled away, he was fairly sure she was sure. But he very gently kissed the bruising, making sure not to hurt her.

She smiled. 'You're just a softie at heart, aren't you?'

He growled as his erection pressed against her core. 'Soft?'

'Hard. So hard.' Her body tensed as she moaned and writhed against him, her hands sliding into his hair. 'God, that's so…good.'

'Yes. It is. But actually…' He slipped his hands behind her knees and picked her up.

She screeched. 'Lewis Parry, what the actual hell?'

'Got to do this properly.' It wasn't exactly far. Three strides and he was laying her down on the plush, soft comforter, her hair splayed on his pillow, copper against white. Just as he remembered. Just as he'd dreamt of so many times.

He lay next to her, propped his head up on his hand and cupped her face for more kisses. He untied the robe and let the fabric fall open. Emotion caught in his throat. 'You are so beautiful, Charlie.'

She smiled at him. 'I want to see you too. All of you.'

He knelt and reached for the hem of his T-shirt but she stopped him. 'Wait. I want to undress you.'

'Be my guest.' He laughed, but then stopped as he watched her still trembling hands tug at the hem.

'You sure you're okay, Charlie?'

'I'm better than okay. I'm just… I don't know. Nervous. Excited.'

'It's me—no need to be nervous.'

'But we've both changed so much over five years. Oh, Lewis, when I think about how much we've missed out on—'

'Don't.' He interrupted her. 'Don't over-think. Just go with this.'

'Intense sexual craving, right?' She knelt up, tugged his T-shirt over his head then ran her fingertips across his chest. 'Wow. You've kept up the gym work, then?'

Pride punched his gut. Okay, yes, he shouldn't care how he looked, but he liked that she still found his hard-worked-for body sexy. She traced over his nipples and giggled when he winced. 'Still ticklish?'

'I guess so.' But his throat was dry and he wasn't laughing any more. The atmosphere was too thick with need, their scent and…anticipation. As her fingers explored his pecs, making her way south towards his erection, he hauled in a stuttering breath, trying hard to rein in the overwhelm of pure lust. He wanted her so much that, if those fingers went anywhere near his groin, he'd explode. So he gently pushed her back on the bed and kissed her again, tracing his own fingertip path down her belly.

He slid his fingers between her legs and she gasped. 'Yes. Yes.'

He slipped his fingers inside her, revelling in her pleasure as she rocked against his hand. A few thrusts had her arching her back, guttural moans filling the room. He found her nub and rubbed slowly.

'Oh. Oh, please, Lewis. I need you. Now…' she managed through snatched, breathless kisses. He felt her tighten, stroking her to a wonderful hot, slick mess of moaning.

'Whoa. You really do want it.'

'Yes. Now.' But then she was pulsing around his fingers and kissing him greedily. 'Please.'

He held her as her orgasm rocked through her, waiting until she rode the crescendo. He kissed her long and hard. But she reached for him and stroked his length, and he held his breath, garnering whatever flimsy thread of control he had left.

'Condom….wallet….' He shook his head then smacked the bed with his palm. 'Damn. They've probably expired.' He grimaced and explained, 'It's been a while.'

But she beamed up at him and stroked his cheek. 'Hey, have you forgotten? There's zero chance of pregnancy. And I haven't had sex with anyone for a long time. Not…since you. I'm good.'

Not since him… His heart squeezed. And *God*, yes—no babies. That had been the core of their problem. But this was now, this was new. 'It's been a long while for me too.'

She pulled him closer and rubbed her wet heat against his erection. 'I want you inside me. I want you, Lewis.'

And he couldn't hold back any longer. He rolled on top of her and gently pushed her legs apart, positioning himself at her entrance. Then he nudged inside her.

God. She was so ready for him. So...*much.* He inhaled sharply and withdrew because it was too much, too fast.

'No! Don't stop.' She moaned. 'Please.'

He thrust into her again, deeper, harder.

'Yes. Please.' She wrapped her legs around his backside, ramping up the rhythm with the rock of her hips. 'This is so good.'

He brushed her damp hair from her face and kissed her. Their gazes locked and he slowed the rhythm. He couldn't take his eyes from her. She was achingly beautiful and here in his arms. She stared up at him as if he was a freaking god or something—the way she used to, back when they'd had so much future to look forward to.

When they could make each other feel this good, how had it all gone so wrong?

Tears slipped down her cheek.

'Hey.' He kissed them away one by one. 'Don't cry. This is...perfect. You are perfect, Charlie.

You're beautiful. *Man*, you are so beautiful, it makes my heart hurt.'

'Oh, Lewis.' She gripped him and hiccupped out a sob, then laughed...all of which mirrored the same confused emotions whirling round his body. She fisted the tears away. 'I'm sorry, I can't help it. It's just, I never thought this could happen. It's so good. I love the way you feel inside me. But it's all just so much.'

'I know. I know. I know.' He pressed his lips to her cheek, then captured her mouth in a searing hot kiss as he thrust into her, faster and harder. Bright light flashed in front of his eyes, in his brain, in his body.

'Lewis.'

He'd never thought he'd hear his name on her lips again.

'Lewis. Yes… *Yes...*' Her tears were coming thick and fast now as he felt her clench and contract around him, then shudder her release in a cry. And his world balled tight into this moment, this woman—this beautiful, amazing woman taking him over the edge too.

For a few long minutes he lay there, cradling her in his arms, dazed, satisfied and happy for the first time in a very long time. It wasn't that they'd rewound, but that they'd built something new out of intense sorrow and confusion.

'Lewis, I'm sorry.' She kept her arms around him, holding him tightly against her. 'I'm sorry.'

He didn't know what she meant. Sorry that she was crying? Sorry that she'd left? Sorry that she'd come back and tipped his world upside down?

But he held her tight and stroked her hair, feeling her heat, feeling her chest heave against him, the wet of her tears on his arm. Then slowly... slowly...she settled. But he kept on holding her closely, not wanting to let her go. *Again.*

She was back and somehow he'd allowed her to creep under his skin, to make him want her, to hope for things they couldn't have—impossible dreams. A future? That was crazy talk, after everything they'd been through before.

And yet...his heart couldn't separate this feeling from the feeling he'd had before it had all started going wrong.

Hope.

He knew then without a doubt that he was going to lose his heart to her all over again.

If he didn't do something about it...fast.

CHAPTER TEN

HOTEL ROOMS HAD always meant sex.

It hadn't felt like *just* sex, though. It had felt consequential in some way: meaningful.

She'd cried, for God's sake. It had all been too much for her poor heart to take. It seemed unreal, as if their problems, their divorce, had somehow magically fallen away.

And yet she couldn't allow any wishful thinking here. She couldn't let this be more than two people having a good time for one night. She couldn't pretend that the last five years hadn't happened—she had left him and broken both their hearts. She'd sent him papers to sign. She'd cried her heart out every night for eighteen months.

It was six-forty-two in the morning and the summer sun was already peeping through the blinds. Charlie had fallen asleep snuggled into the crook of Lewis's arm—fitting exactly the way she'd fitted before—a deep, satisfying sleep that she hadn't experienced for a long time. Then she'd woken suddenly, not quite sure where she was.

When reality hit, guilt did too. She should be with Lucy, not there. She'd got carried away with her own needs and wants instead of putting her sister first.

Should she sneak out and leave him sleeping? His eyes were closed, his long, dark lashes something any woman would be envious of. His hair was tousled. Would he be as confused as she was? She could leave now and avoid what could be an embarrassing conversation trawling through regret and recrimination about being here together. Although she'd had the best time, and would not regret that one night with Lewis.

'Morning,' he whispered against her throat as his warm hand snaked across her naked belly. He tugged her closer to him, her back tight against his chest, spooning her. 'You slept.'

She relaxed back against the pillows. There was no sneaking out now. 'I did.'

'You also snored.' He laughed.

She pushed back gently against his shoulder. 'I did not.'

'Okay, more a purr than a snore. But you were out like a light.'

She turned over, about to say she was going to grab a shower and head off, but he smiled, and her belly quivered and tingled in response. She would not regret last night. And she could not resist him now. 'I need to go…soon.'

'I know.' His nose wrinkled as he pulled a face.

It made good sense to leave now; it would alleviate some of her guilt if she got home this early in the morning, and hopefully found her sister and niece still sleeping, and it would give her much-needed emotional space to work out exactly what she felt about making love with Lewis.

But she did not want to leave. 'Maybe in five minutes?'

He edged away a little. 'Look, if you need to go, that's fine.'

'Whoa. Are you trying to get rid of me?' *God*, he regretted this. He regretted her staying.

But he frowned and shook his head. 'Of course not. I just know you want to get back to Lucy.' He raised himself up on his elbow, threading his fingers through her hair and rubbing a strand against his cheek. 'You know, I always loved your hair. I'm glad you didn't change it or dye it some random colour.'

Was he remembering their wedding night too, when he'd unclipped her hair, let it fall over her shoulders, nuzzled his face into it and told her how much he loved her? She'd forgotten how much he'd adored her hair back then. 'I've been sorely tempted to change it over the years. This colour runs in the family. Stella's got it too.' She grimaced. 'Poor kid.'

'Why? It's the most beautiful colour I've ever seen.'

'Not when you're in primary school and everyone calls you Carrot Top and other less nice nicknames. It's the kind of colour you grow into and only appreciate when you're older.'

'Tell me who they were and I'll… I'll sort them out for calling you names.' He flexed his biceps. 'I have a certain set of skills.'

'Sort them out? No need, Mr Bodyguard. Stand down.' She stroked his arm, laughing. 'I love it now and I don't care what anyone thinks.'

But with the thought of Stella her chest constricted and she wriggled out from under his arm. 'Look, I do really need to get back. Lucy… She pretends she's okay…'

Like you always did.

When would people start to treat her as if she was a grown adult and start being honest with her? When would they stop protecting her and let her protect them for a change? 'But I want to take the burden off her.'

'Sure.' He jumped out of bed and slipped on the robe she'd been wearing last night. 'Coffee first; I know you don't like to function without it.'

'You remember! I *can't* function without it.' She laughed. 'I need it IV'd in the mornings.'

He fiddled with the chrome coffee machine, then peered at the selection of purple, silver and gold coffee pods. 'Coming up. Hop in the shower and it'll be ready when you're done. You want me to give you a ride home?'

'That would be great. Thanks.'

Was he in a hurry to get rid of her—just being

polite about the coffee and the shower when he really wanted her gone?

She went through to the bathroom and turned on the shower. Two minutes on her own, and she was immediately hit with all the questions she'd wilfully ignored last night.

A ride home…and then what? What did this mean? Were they back together? No. That would be…difficult, given what they'd been through before. The warm water didn't help soothe her confusion. Did it have to mean anything? It could just be two consenting adults having fun.

But then what?

Last night the answer to that question hadn't seemed important, but today she needed certainty. Oh, she was no good at this. How could she pretend it had just been casual sex when…well… when her heart's reaction was far from casual?

She dried and dressed in yesterday's clothes, used the hotel's freebie toothbrush and paste then went back into the main room. He was sitting at the coffee table, looking at his phone.

Her heart danced just to look at him. What was he thinking?

He looked up and pointed at two steaming cups of coffee. 'There you go. Ambrosia from the gods.'

'Thanks.' She grabbed a cup and had a sip. 'What have you got planned today? Anything fun?'

He glanced back at his phone. 'Just messaging Logan. I'm going to the beach with him and the family, then lunch at their place in Meadow-bank. It's a sort of tradition now, whenever I get the weekend off—which isn't often. We hang out, and sometimes I even babysit.'

'It sounds lovely. It's good that you two are so close.' He had made his brother's family, his own family. Made up for the lack of his own kids. Which, despite him being at odds to tell her it wasn't her fault, it was. And all of a sudden she felt a little *lost*….robbed, even…because she couldn't pretend they didn't have a break-up history mired in her infertility. Or that he still wanted a family she couldn't give him.

She needed to go.

'Okay, do you mind if we make tracks now? I really need to give Lucy a break from parent-ing duties. She needs to get her rest.' To add to the emotional rollercoaster, guilt shimmied down her spine. Being with Lewis, amazing as he was, wasn't what she was supposed to be doing. Lucy would forgive her, right? 'I feel bad about staying out overnight.'

He fleetingly frowned. 'Don't. She would have said if she needed you, right?'

'I'm not so sure. You're not the only one who hides their feelings, Lewis.'

'Hey, I'm trying here. You're not the only one who's done a lot of thinking over the last few years, Charlie. And some growing up too.' He ran his hand through his hair and then smiled. But there was something about it that was almost sad, as if he was contemplating something coming to an end. Maybe he was. 'I had a great night, Charlie. I'm glad you're back.'

Okay... This new honest and open Lewis, the Lewis who told her what he wanted and needed, was someone else—interesting and refreshing and so not what he used to be like. And yet she was waiting for the 'but', which should be a relief and would make things less difficult. But... at the same time...she liked him. Last night had been amazing.

Oh, she was all kinds of confused. 'I'm not sure you were very glad when you found me in that smashed-up car.'

'Okay, I'll admit I was shocked.' He laughed. 'And I understand about Lucy. She's the big sister, right? She feels responsible—like Logan does with me. Only thirty minutes' difference but sometimes he acts like it's thirty years.'

'She's always looked out for me, and has been one of my fiercest supporters. I think I took it for granted, *expected* the support even. It was too easy for me not to stand on my own two feet because I had my parents, Lucy and you to do the hard yards for me.'

'Hey, you got the brilliant exam results, not us.' He drained his cup.

'But you made sure I had nothing else to worry

about. You made food or my parents brought us food parcels. My mother paid a cleaner every week to come spruce the house. I was a spoilt princess.'

'You weren't.' He cleared the empty coffee cups onto a little tray and carried them to the console. 'You were studying and learning your new job. It's not easy being a junior doctor.'

'Oh, I was spoilt, Lewis. I was also selfish and a little bit lazy. I didn't like being pampered by everyone but I couldn't bring myself to take control either. Then, when I moved to London, I... Well, I pushed *everyone* away—not just you. I only came back twice in five years and even then only briefly. I wouldn't even let my family visit me in London.' And she'd felt so very alone, but hadn't had any energy to give to anyone else, to answer their questions or even have a conversation about what was going on inside her head and her heart.

He leaned back against the console, legs crossed at the ankles. 'I had no idea. Why?'

'I don't know for sure. I think I needed some distance from everyone. Some space from everything I knew—a new direction. A new life with no pain in it. No reminder of what I couldn't do or who I was.' Until she'd realised she couldn't run away from herself or her feelings. She'd had to face them. 'But, again selfishly, didn't think how that might have affected my mum and dad. And Lucy.'

LOUISA GEORGE 133

'You're being very hard on yourself. You'd been through a very difficult time; you were all over the place emotionally. I'm sure they understood.'

'I didn't give them a choice. But I can imagine how hurt they must have felt and worried about my mental wellbeing. I only stayed in cursory contact when necessary for the first couple of years. When Lucy called to tell me about her pregnancy, I didn't rush home to be with her for the birth; I just sent flowers and cooed over video calls. I missed some of Stella's firsts, and didn't help in those difficult early days. I wasn't here when Lucy found the lump. She didn't tell anyone until after Mum and Dad went away to do their charity work. She was facing all that on her own. There was a chasm between us and it was my fault.' Now it was time for her to give back. 'I'm trying to make amends for that.'

'I'm sure you don't need to. I am absolutely sure Lucy understands you just needed some alone time.' He smiled. 'But, what are you waiting for? Get your bag. I'll take you.'

'I can get a bus if you need to get to Logan's.'

He frowned. 'We're neighbours, remember? I won't let you get the bus when I practically drive past your house. I have to change and grab Lola's present anyway.'

'Oh, okay. If you insist.' She grabbed her bag, not ready for this intimate time with him to end, because she had no idea how they would navigate the 'what next?'

Twenty minutes later, they pulled up outside Lucy's home and Lewis twisted in his seat to talk to Charlie. The conversation from the hotel had been sparse and the atmosphere a little loaded, as if they both knew they needed to say something but didn't know what.

'Right, here you go.' He rubbed the back of his neck. 'Um… What do we do now?'

Awkward.

'I don't know. I came here to look after Lucy and Stella and then somehow here I am, doing the drive of shame.' She looked down at yesterday's clothes, and felt a belt of contrition tightening around her chest, but smiled nonetheless.

He stroked her hair, then palmed her cheek. 'Hey. There's absolutely nothing to be ashamed of. We're consenting adults. We were married once.' What had he said last night about grown adults and sexual craving? But there was something in his expression that gave her pause before he added, 'How about we catch up when we're both ready?'

What? When? Wasn't he ready either? Did he feel the same discombobulation?

Suddenly she felt a little out of her depth. They'd spent an intense few hours getting to the core of what had split them up, but they certainly weren't healed enough to lay their hearts wide open yet.

And she shouldn't be doing this when she had so little time to give. It wasn't fair on him or on Lucy.

And it wasn't fair on her own heart. She didn't want to fall for him again and then lose him. She'd barely recovered from that before. 'Sure. Yes. I'm in a difficult space at the moment.'

'I get it: Lucy; Stella; the job… It's a lot. No problem. You know where I am and you have my phone number if you need me. But, in the meantime, no doubt I'll see you at work.' He nodded.

And she'd have the tease and temptation of seeing him…probably on every shift, trying to ignore the ache, the want and the need. But neither of them was in a position to make more of this. She sighed as her chest constricted. 'So, you're okay with this? You know…not making plans? Please—tell me the truth.'

He smiled wryly. 'Hey, don't stress. I have to get my head straight too. I did not expect any of last night to ever happen, so I'm just sort of…working through it. But, for the record, I had a good time—*great* time. And I'd like us to be friends, if that works for you.'

'Friends. Sure, I can do that.'

And wow: *just sort of working through it.* His honesty about his feelings was coming thick and fast. She squeezed his hand, but when he leaned in to kiss her cheek she turned her mouth to meet his. She couldn't resist kissing him again.

He hesitated, then groaned as their lips met.

And, oh, how her body heated and responded to his kiss.

It was a while before they came up for air.

She chuckled, more in embarrassment at her lack of restraint than anything else. 'Okay, sorry. That was a very un-friend thing to do. But I couldn't resist just one last kiss. Right; friends from now?'

He chuckled, his eyes still filled with heat. 'Yeah. Friends from now. You want to synchronise watches or something?'

'No need; I think I'm good now. Right, I should go.' She opened the door and climbed out, but leaned back in through the window to add, 'I'll see you…some time. Thanks for a great night.'

'Yeah. Back at ya, Charlie.' He leaned across the passenger seat and smiled up at her.

Oh, those eyes. That mouth. That man.

Last night.

This kiss.

Oh, hell…the friend thing wasn't working very well at all.

CHAPTER ELEVEN

IT WAS A great night, Lewis thought as he jogged down the path to the beach. *Pinch me.*

Had it really happened—Charlie back in his arms? After their deep and raw conversation, so many emotions had been swimming through his veins. He hadn't been so honest or felt so close to anyone for a long time. Sex had been the natural conclusion—inevitable after that first stolen kiss.

And now what?

He wasn't sure how to navigate casual sex with his ex, or just being friends, or how to protect himself from falling for her again. Because, even though they'd straddled some of the niggly reasons why they'd split, some issues were still there, right? Big issues too. Besides, she'd made it clear she didn't want anything deep or involved.

So why the hell had he allowed last night to happen?

He spotted the girls in bright-pink bathers paddling in the shallows, with Logan helicoptering over them. Lewis watched them splash each other for a moment with a sting in his chest. Lucky Logan; he'd got it all: a lovely wife and three gorgeous kids. Lewis was thrilled for him; he was. After what they'd been through growing up, his brother deserved every scrap of happiness, every moment of family life with his precious girls.

But it didn't stop him craving that for himself, even now.

His brother met him with a bro hug of hand-slap and back-clap. 'Hey, you look bright-eyed and bushy-tailed. Early night?'

'Hmm.' Far from it, but he wasn't sure what to say. As far as Logan was concerned, Charlie had abandoned her husband…just like everyone else had over their early years. Logan was a stickler for staying and trying to work things through, just like Lewis. And Lewis hadn't yet found the head space or opportunity to tell Logan that Charlotte Rose was back.

Logan frowned at Lewis's non-committal response. 'What did you do, watch the game? Shame about the result, eh? It was a lousy night to be out anyway. There was flash-flooding on Tamaki Drive. You wouldn't think so now, though. It's a beaut of a day.'

Flash-flooding florecast.

God, she was beautiful. And his head was a mess. Images from last night kept flashing through his brain: her mouth; her smile; the tight press of her body. 'Actually, I went out with Charlie.'

Logan stepped back, almost falling over a sand castle, then stepped down into a deep hole. He staggered, then fell backwards onto the sand. 'Charlie? Your Charlie? Dr Charlie? Your wife?'

'Ex-wife.' Lewis held out his hand and hauled Logan upright.

Logan brushed the sand from his shorts. 'How? Why?'

'She's moved back to Auckland and we bumped into each other at work.'

Logan's eyes roamed Lewis face, assessing. 'And…?'

Siblings—they always wanted a piece of you. 'We had dinner.'

'So you're getting back together? Just like that?'

'We had dinner, Logan.' And great sex. 'No one said anything about getting back together.'

'Okay.' Logan's eyebrows rose and he blew out a slow breath. 'How was she? How are you?'

He thought of her underneath him—the way she'd looked at him as he'd entered her; the way she'd clung to him. The way tears had slipped down her cheeks, emotion spilling over. 'She's great, actually. Really good.'

'And you?' Logan peered closer at him. 'You look too happy about it and that gives me the hee-bie-jeebies.'

Lewis inhaled deeply. Happy? Confused, more like. 'Yeah. I'm not gonna lie. It was a shock to see her at first but we talked and…well… I'm okay… I think. We agreed to try be friends, seeing as we're likely going to be working together on occasion.'

'Friends?' His brother's eyes widened in shock. 'Be careful, bro. I remember how you were after she'd gone. I don't ever want to see you like that again.'

Lewis remembered too and no way was he going back to that darkness again. 'Don't worry, I can handle it. I'm in a good space now.'

'Yes. And it's good to see.' Logan shook his head and put his hand on Lewis's shoulder. 'But, with Charlie back, how long is that going to last?'

He had a point. Lewis had been broken into a million pieces when she'd left. 'I'm being careful. We're both older and wiser.' *Liar*. Last night he'd felt like a giddy teenager again, carried away with wild need.

'Do you...you know...?' Logan inhaled as his question trailed off.

'Know what?' Lewis frowned at his brother. Where was this going?

'Still love her?'

'Whoa. Get straight to the point, why don't you?' But Logan had always talked about how he was feeling. He didn't hold back. He was open and honest; Lewis had got the other side of that coin. He preferred to keep everything inside so he could work it through. And, anyway, no one had ever cared what he thought about stuff. If he'd had a problem and wanted help from an adult, he might as well have shouted into the wind.

Except for Charlie... She'd pushed him to say

things. And he was trying. He just wasn't sure if he trusted himself, or her…although after last night he wasn't sure. She hadn't given him false hope or led him on. They'd both consented and parted in agreement.

It had been a good night. He wanted to do it again.

But did he still *love* her? Absolutely not. She'd thrashed his heart. He couldn't do that to himself, never again.

Logan was still looking at him, waiting for a response. Lewis shook his head. 'Come on, man. It was one night.'

'Night?' His brother glared at him. 'You said dinner.'

Great. There was no getting out of this. 'We got caught in the rain doing a resus on some poor bloke who got run over in the middle of Quay Street, and then she couldn't get a taxi, and I had that hotel room booked…' He shrugged. Yeah, it did sound a likely story, now he thought about it, but he wasn't going to lie. 'So she spent the night, okay? It was probably closure for both of us. One night, then we can both properly move on.'

Because, in reality, it looked as if he hadn't fully moved on at all, no matter how much he told himself he had. He was healed, yes, but he hadn't been able to find happiness with anyone else.

Logan shot him a blunt look and was about to

say something when Lily hurtled towards them. 'Uncle Lewis, piggy-back ride?'

'Please,' admonished Logan.

Lily beamed her toothy smile. '*Please,* Uncle Lewis?'

How could he resist? This could be the only chance at a family he ever got, these little poppets in pink. Plus, maybe it'd get him back in the good books with his brother. He bent down onto all fours. 'Okay, hop on, both of you. And be nice to each other.'

The little girls giggled and screeched as they scrambled onto his back with Lily in front and Lola at the back, complaining about being behind her little sister and giggling at the same time.

He crawled across the sand, ignoring the burn in his knees and palms…and in his heart. This was everything he'd dreamt of happening with Charlie: two little copper-headed kids, squirming and wriggling and laughing. Then Sunday lunch all together, maybe with Logan and his brood too—family time.

Charlie had thought that impossible and he'd been too distraught to argue. But there were options, right? Why hadn't they talked about adoption or surrogacy? Why had he been so closed to that idea five years ago?

But how could they talk about that now? They weren't in that space. She'd drawn her boundary and he had to respect that. Hell, he needed that line in the sand too.

So why the hell was he imagining happy families when nothing could be further from reality?

'Hey, there,' Charlie whispered as she opened the door to Lucy's bedroom to find her niece asleep on her sister's chest. Lucy's eyes were closed as she lay on the bed, her chest steadily rising and falling. She looked peaceful, which was lovely, given the stress she was under right now.

Charlie's heart squeezed. These two here were what was important. *But, oops...*

Charlie tiptoed backwards and closed the door as quietly as she could.

'Charlie? Charlotte, is that you?' came a strained whisper.

Charlie opened the door again and popped her head round. 'Hey, yes. Sorry, I didn't mean to disturb you.'

'Oh, don't worry. She's been napping for an hour now so it's probably time she woke up.' Lucy looked down at her daughter and smiled that soft mamma smile filled with adoration. 'She had a restless night.'

Charlie's chest ached with guilt. 'Oh, I'm sorry, I should have been here.'

'No, you should not. I told you to go. The least I can do is let you have a night out every now and then.'

Which did not erase the guilt at all. 'How are you feeling?'

'Yuck.' Lucy sat up, leaning back against the pillows, and hoisted a fast-asleep Stella higher on her chest. She looked worn out, but she smiled. 'But I don't want to talk about me. I want every little detail about your illicit night.'

To be honest, Charlie didn't know what to say, or how to feel. 'Oh, you know? It was nice.'

Lucy guffawed. 'You stay at a fabulous hotel with a gorgeous man and it's *nice*?'

'Well, we did have a medical emergency to deal with as well.' Her sex-induced tachycardia, as well as poor Graham.

Lucy rolled her eyes. 'Yeah, yeah. And it was raining and all the apps were down and there was absolutely nothing you could do except go to his hotel.' Lucy smiled softly. 'So what happened?'

Charlie shook her head and glanced down at her sleeping niece. 'No can do. Stella is far too young to hear this.'

'Oh? That good?'

Charlie plopped down on the bed next to her sister. 'Yes. *That* good.'

Lucy peered more closely at Charlie's face. 'And yet, you don't seem your usually happy self.'

Charlie pressed her lips together, because she was smiling inside; she really was. It had been un-freaking-believable but tinged now with 'what next?' and guilt at not being here. 'I'm not sure where we're at.'

'You're seeing him again?' Lucy frowned at Charlie's shrug. 'You're not seeing him again?'

'Undoubtedly I'll see him again. He brings in my patients. Our paths will cross many, many times.' The enormity of the potential emotional and personal fallout from last night finally hit her. Making love had muddied everything: distracted her from her commitment to looking after her family members; intruded into her work space and bruised her heart. 'We're friends, apparently. He's working things through.'

Lucy's eyes widened. 'He said that?'

'Yeah. But anyway…it doesn't matter. It's not a good time for me.'

Lucy's frown deepened. 'Because of me? Please don't let me stop you having fun. Watching you living a great life might be the only good thing I have left, after this little one, of course.' She kissed the top of her daughter's head.

'No.' Tears pricked Charlie's eyes. 'Don't say that.'

'It's true. We have to face up to it. My life is crappy and horrible and I'm scared to death. Let's just hope the medicine is working, okay?'

Charlie nodded and squeezed her sister's hand. 'Absolutely. It will. It *will*.'

'And I don't want to talk about it any more. It's all I ever seem to think about and it's not good for me. I need a distraction and, unfortunately for you, you're it.'

Lucy cupped Charlie's face with her Stella-free hand and sighed. 'I know this thing with Lewis is complicated; you have so much history. And I do not want you hurting like you did before or scurrying away overseas again. I should be telling you to be careful. To take your time. To figure out what *you* want. If it's just that one night, then great, you can tick that box. If it's more, then, you'll have to talk to him about it. Tell him what you want. Find out what he wants.'

'The same as he always did—kids.' Charlie exhaled slowly.

'So you talked about it?'

'No. But he's so close with Logan's girls. It's obvious.'

I was gutted, if I'm honest. Absolutely broken. His words rubbed a bruise in her chest wall.

'I don't suppose you talked about other options? Adoption? Fostering?'

'It wasn't that kind of conversation, Luce.'

Lucy brushed Charlotte's hair back from her forehead and smiled softly. 'Oh, sweetheart, I'm sorry.'

'Because, if he doesn't want that, we'd still have

the same issues as before and I'm not ready to be rejected. Anyway, it was one night, Lucy. You are my number one focus.' She wrapped Lucy and Stella in a warm hug. 'Other than to see you get better, I have no idea what I want.'

How about a carefree, problem-free, happy, committed relationship with a gorgeous man? Lots of kids. *Love*.

'I don't want a life without you,' he'd said on their wedding night.

Yet he'd managed just fine—was thriving, in fact.

While her heart, it seemed, was still a fractured mess.

CHAPTER TWELVE

'THIS IS TIA, a twenty-seven-year-old woman who fell off her horse when she was trying to do a jump at speed. She fell forward over the horse's head; face and head took the brunt of the impact, as you can see by the grazing and swelling on her forehead and bruising around the eyes. Luckily, she was wearing a helmet, but a witness said she was possibly unconscious for a few minutes. Glasgow coma scale was thirteen on initial assessment but fifteen now.' Lewis glanced up at the group of medics he was handing over to and momentarily froze.

He hadn't seen Charlie come in. He certainly hadn't realised she was standing right in front of him, her startling blue eyes watching him as she listened intently. Her hair was piled on top of her head in a gorgeously messy bun with stray, loose tendrils framing her pretty face. Lip gloss highlighted her perfect Cupid's bow. His brain immediately rewound to the night in the hotel: the heat, the touch, the intensity of it all; the honesty.

No.

He shook himself. He was not going there. He

was doing his job. Charlie was a friend, that was all. 'She also has swelling and pain in her upper right arm, right hip and right knee. She's had ketorolac for pain relief, which is working well.'

'Hi, Tia. My name is Charlie. I'm one of the doctors here. Good to hear Lewis's magic medicine is working.' Charlie flashed him a smile that reached deep into his heart and tugged it in a way not so much friendly, more sexy, then fixed back on their patient. 'I'll need to ask you a few more questions and examine you again, so I'm sorry if it seems as if we're repeating ourselves.'

He stepped back and let her do her stuff. He couldn't begin to count how many handovers he'd given over the course of his career, but he'd felt like a blathering idiot every time he'd done one in front of Charlie in the past few days.

He was so aware of her. Aware of her eyes on him and of the memories from years ago bolstered by the memories of Saturday night. Memories of the mind-blowing kisses, and her beautiful naked body. Of him finally opening up, as if a pressure valve had been released inside him, giving him hope and making him…what? *Exposed*. All of these messy emotions didn't stop him doing his job—he'd never let anything get in the way of that—but they didn't make it easy.

He stepped away out of the cubicle, eager to put distance between himself and his ex-wife. Maybe one day he would come to work and feel platonic vibes about her.

Today was not that day.

Keen to leave, Lewis found Brin at the nurses' station, chatting to some of the medical team. 'Hey, Brin, ready to go?'

Brin nodded. 'Sure. But I'm parched and it's my turn for coffees again. So, I'll go grab them and meet you in the van.'

'Great.' That would give Lewis some time to breathe and get his head straight after seeing Charlie. He turned to leave but came face to face with her as she stepped out from behind the cubicle curtain.

She looked surprised and a little embarrassed now it was just the two of them. She gave him a half-smile. She was guarded, unsure. 'Hey... um...friend.'

'Hey, Charlie. How's things?' Was it his imagination or had there been extra emphasis on the word 'friend', as if she was feeling the same discombobulation he was? The memory of their night together filled the air, unacknowledged, loaded.

'Good.' She nodded. 'Yes. I'm good.'

He waited for her to ask him how he was, but nothing came, so he said, 'And Lucy? Stella?'

'They're okay.'

'Right. Good.' He wasn't sure what to say next. She wasn't exactly encouraging conversation but she wasn't making moves to leave either. They'd shared a very intimate night together... hell, a marriage of four years and longer than that in a relationship... but friends? It seemed it didn't come naturally. Maybe they couldn't have a relationship that didn't involve the emotional and physical. *Ouch.* That didn't bode well for their future professional relationship.

Because what he wanted was to whip her into his arms and kiss her right here in the emergency room. Take her to his bed and make long, slow, sweet love to her. Wake up with her in the morning, lots of mornings.... *Every* morning...

Hot damn. He couldn't let these emotions take hold. He shoved his hands into his pockets and rocked back on his heels, trying to be nonchalant when his body felt the opposite. 'Cool. Well, I should be going.'

'Yeah. Me too.' But she paused, a smile flickering as something seemed to occur to her. 'Oh, I almost forgot. Did you hear about Graham?'

'Graham?' For a moment he was confused, then he realised. 'Oh, yes, our CPR man. No, I haven't had the chance to ask after him.'

'He's actually hanging in there. In Intensive Care, but improving. Apparently, it was touch and go for a while, but he pulled through. We did good, Lewis.'

And, with that, the tension between them seemed to diminish. Maybe it was because they were in safe territory talking about work. Or maybe because they'd been reminded of how good they could be together. 'That's great news. I'm so pleased. I might pop up to see him if I get a chance.'

'Yeah.' She nodded, her eyes brighter now. 'Just goes to show that things don't always end up the way you think they might.'

Tell that to my pathetic, hopeful heart.

'Go us.' He raised his palm and she high-fived it.

'The dream team.' Her smile was worth all the awkward tension.

'Hey, you two.' Brin was striding towards them carrying two takeaway cups. 'I've just had Mia on the phone and she wondered if you'd like to come for a barbecue at the weekend?'

Lewis wasn't sure whether Brin meant the two of them generally or *together*. His meddling was getting a little out of control. He glanced at Charlie, and she looked as uncomfortable as he felt at the invitation, so before he replied Lewis narrowed his eyes in a question to his colleague. 'What's the occasion?'

Brin rolled his eyes. 'Sorry, should have been clearer—house warming. It's a little overdue, but Mia's sister-in-law and family are coming over for the weekend, so we thought it'd be a good opportunity to throw a party.'

Which meant there'd be others there, it wouldn't be just a double date kind of thing. Lewis exhaled and agreed to come, because refusing the invita-

tion would be out of character and would probably engender more questions from his co-worker,
not fewer. 'Sure thing, sounds good. Let me know
what to bring.'

But Charlie shook her head. 'No, sorry. Thanks,
anyway, but I need to look after Lucy.'

Brin frowned. 'Your daughter?'

'Sister.' She smiled tightly. At the mention of
Lucy, her body language had become guarded and
taut. Looking after her family was taking a toll
and Lewis wondered how he could ease that burden. Then he remembered he was not getting involved.

Brin smiled. 'No worries. Bring her too.'

'Okay, I'll ask her. Thanks.' Charlie's gaze
darted to Lewis. It seemed she was checking if
that was okay by him. He nodded. He could hardly
refuse, could he? She looked back at Brin. 'She's
got a baby, six months old: is it okay to bring her
too?'

Brin grinned. 'That's no problem. Mia loves
babies. We've got a little one too. Bring them all.
The more the merrier. Stay an hour, stay all evening, whatever works.' Brin nodded at Lewis and
handed him a warm takeaway cup. 'Okay, boss.
I'll be in the van clearing up. Take your time.'

As they watched him walk away, Lewis heaved
a sigh. 'Geez, I am so sorry about him.'

She laughed. 'It's fine. He's just being friendly.'

'Or meddling. Looks like we're not going to be let out of this. You good with it?'

'Yes. I guess. It's actually nice to be invited out somewhere and hopefully make some friends. I haven't had much of a chance to meet many people or catch up with my old Auckland mates.' Her eyebrows rose and he wondered if she was alluding to *their* old Auckland mates, joint school friends with whom she'd lost touch with living so far away, while he'd done his best to stay in contact. She shrugged. 'I'll ask Lucy to come, because she could use cheering up. With the chemo, she's not keen on going out and mingling too much. Her immune system's not great.'

'I could pick you all up...' The words were out of his mouth before he realised what he was saying. Not only would he be up close with Charlie in a car, but he'd have to see Lucy again after the messy divorce from her little sister. How would he navigate that? But he couldn't sit by and see them worry or struggle when he might be able to help somehow. 'It would save you driving your little broken car or using public transport, which is a greater risk for catching infections. And if it's all too much for her then I can run her home any time, no worries.'

Her smile widened. 'That would be lovely.'

'That's what friends are for, right?' This time he made himself *feel* the emphasis on the word 'friend'.

'Yeah. I guess.' She put her hand on his arm, sending sparks of need firing across his skin, arrowing to his chest and lower…way lower. He thought about the way she tasted, and the soft sounds she'd made when he'd slid inside her, and the sparks in his belly threatened to burst into flame. 'Thanks, Lewis.'

He tried to push back all sexy thoughts of her. 'No worries. I just have to put on my big boy pants to face your older sister. Otherwise, everything is golden.'

'She won't bite.' She chuckled. 'She always liked you. She knows I was the one who left.'

'Hmm. The jury's still out on that. You were heartbroken and I couldn't fix it. That was my job, right?' He imagined what Logan might say whenever—*if ever*—he got to see Charlie again.

'Oh, Lewis, it was never your job to fix my broken heart. I'm responsible for my own emotions.' She patted his arm and he realised just how much she'd changed in the intervening years since their break-up. Back then, she'd have allowed him to wade in and try to fix everything. Now she was self-determined and fiercely autonomous. It suited her, a lot. She grinned. 'Don't worry. If I say you're generously being our taxi driver, she'll be fine with it. She just wants me to be happy.'

'And are you?' It was the million-dollar question. It was probably unfair to ask, really, given what she was going through.

She closed her eyes briefly, then exhaled long and slowly. 'That's too big a question for work time. I'm loving spending time with my family. I have a great job and…ahem…*interesting* friends and colleagues.' She shot him a knowing smile. 'But ask me again in a few months, when Lucy's treatment's finished. That's all I can think of at the moment. When she gets the all-clear, I'll be deliriously happy.'

If ever there was a sign they needed to be platonic more than ever, this was it. Because he realised he wanted her to say, yes, she was happy they'd spent the night together. That they'd found each other again. That there was still something between them. Which was pathetic wishful thinking on his part, and also very selfish. Charlie was conflicted and busy and had other people she needed to put ahead of herself, and therefore ahead of him. He nodded. 'Sure. I get it.'

'And I mean thanks for understanding, Lewis. For sticking to the plan. You know…being friends. Not asking for more. And, on the other hand, for not ghosting me. I'm not sure which would be harder to deal with.' Her hand was still on his arm and the way she was looking at him, as if she was truly grateful, made him want to wrap his arms round her and hold her close. To soothe her worries and make her feel better. But that wasn't his job any more.

'I would never ghost you, Charlie. We're too old and wise to play those kinds of games.' He couldn't help smiling. 'Thank God you're not a mind-reader, is all.'

She blinked, then her smile grew into a grin, sexy and loaded. 'Lewis! Not you too?'

'Me what?' He was all mock-innocence.

She leaned closer so no one else could hear. 'Struggling with the aftermath of the other night?'

'I can't get it out of my head.' This close, he could see deep into her eyes. He saw the tease she was fighting, the need for affection. He was struggling with his need to protect her too, to be the one to solve all her problems and to have the answers. She hadn't wanted them five years ago and she certainly wouldn't want them now. But he couldn't help wanting to erase all her pain.

He needed to keep this growing connection between them under control if he was going to get out whole.

He took a sip of coffee and remembered that Brin was waiting for him. 'Look, I'd better go. Let me know if you want me to pick you all up. Otherwise, I'll see you at Brin's. I'll message you his address.'

Then he flashed her a quick smile and left, balling up his emotions and stuffing them deep inside, exactly where they should have stayed the moment he knew she was back.

* * *

It was silly to be nervous. It was a barbecue—friends from work—that was all.

But, the moment Lewis's car pulled up outside, her heart jumped into a very weird tachycardic rhythm she was fairly sure no cardiologist had ever seen on a heart trace.

Stop it.

As he crunched up the gravel path, she started to feel a little dizzy due to her jumpy heart rate and anticipatory nerves.

Ridiculous.

The rap on the door made her jump, even though she was expecting it.

'Lucy! We're heading off,' she called up the stairs. And received a muffled grunt in return. Then she took a deep breath and opened the door.

Hell... He looked good today in his untucked white linen shirt and duck-egg-blue shorts. His dark hair was casually tousled as always and there was a smattering of stubble on his jaw. His lovely soulful brown eyes glittered as he smiled. 'Taxi for Dr Rose?'

'Hey. Thanks so much for this.'

After holding off asking him to pick them all up, she'd capitulated at Lucy's urging: 'He has a much bigger car and it'll be so much more comfortable for us all.'

That was before Lucy had decided not to join them after all.

Laughing, Charlie hauled the car seat from the ground and handed it to him. 'Could you take this? You have to put the seat belt through the back.'

'Got it.' He grinned. 'Three nieces; I know the drill.' Then he disappeared down the path and into the car. She was mesmerised by the rhythm of his steps, the way he turned and winked at her, as he'd used to when they'd been happily married, and the cute smile that seemed to reach to her uterus and stroked. Which was damned unfair, given she had a non-functioning uterus and no amount of stroking would make it work.

But, oh, he was lovely. Her body prickled with awareness. Was he more lovely now than five years ago? He seemed more centred, wiser, happier in himself. He seemed confident. He was definitely better in so many ways. It was only when he backed out of the back passenger door that she realised she'd been staring at his backside for far longer than anyone would consider acceptable. If staring at a hunk of man's backside was acceptable at all… *Oops.*

'Come on, lovely,' she cooed at little Stella and picked her up from the travel cot they used as a playpen in the lounge. 'Time to be sociable.'

She was glad they were going to be surrounded by friends new to her, so temptation could stay at bay. And also frustrated that they would be surrounded by friends, so temptation could stay at bay. Oh, life was so complicated these days.

She yelled upstairs again. 'Bye, Luce. Please call me if you need anything.'

She waited for a reply. There came some splashing then a long sigh. 'Have fun, girls.'

'Car seat is in,' Lewis said as he walked back up the path. But he frowned as she pulled the door closed behind her. He ran up to take Stella's change bag out of Charlie's hands. 'Hey, give that to me. Where's Lucy?'

'In the bath. And she's not coming out for anyone or anything, apparently.' Charlie giggled. 'She has a glass of her favourite rosé, scented candles, some chocolate-covered ginger and a new romance novel to devour. She's not up to seeing anyone, but she is up to pampering herself. I told her I'd bring Stella with us so she can relax.'

'Great idea.' After he put the changing bag into the car boot, he took Stella from her arms as naturally as anything, then he beamed at the baby, swinging her high in the air until she giggled. 'Hello, little one. Yes, it's me, Lewis. We have met, but you probably don't remember. Yes, that's my chin. Yes, it's scratchy.' He shot Charlie a smile. 'She's a feisty little thing.'

'She needs to be, for her mum's sake.'

'It's difficult, for sure. But she won't understand what's going on.' His smile flattened a little, his eyes filling with warmth and worry. Then he turned another full-beam grin on Stella. 'Okay, missy. Let's get you plugged in so we can all go party.'

Charlie's breath caught in her throat. Lewis was gorgeous when he was just being himself but, smiling and laughing with a baby in his arms, he was devastating.

She'd tried to keep her distance, had not encouraged anything past polite conversation at work. Yet here she was, about to get into a car with him, go to a party and play. Once upon a time, playing with Lewis had been her most favourite thing.

Maybe it still was…

'Hey!' Brin grinned as he tugged open the front door twenty minutes later. 'Come in! Come in! Glad you could make it. Hello, little one.' He tickled Stella under her chin as he walked them through to a bright, smart-looking kitchen. 'This must be…?'

He glanced at Charlie. She smiled and bounced Stella up and down in her arms. 'Stella, my niece.'

'Something you guys have in common, then. Nieces.' Brin threw Lewis a look of encouragement and nodded towards Charlie with raised eyebrows, as if to say, *get in, lad. Make a move.*

She rolled her eyes at Lewis in solidarity. He smiled and mouthed the word, 'Sorry.' Somehow, their joint reaction at Brin's unsubtle matchmaking attempts was bringing them closer together. *Go figure.*

'Girls, yes, so many girls, including your Harper.'

Lewis shook his head as he put a large bowl of delicious-looking caprese salad, gourmet sausages and halloumi cheese onto the kitchen counter. 'Where's Mia, and Harper?'

Brin gestured towards the back door. 'Outside. Come and look at our new back yard, mate. You're going to love it.'

'Huh?' Lewis frowned again and they all followed Brin outside to a neat back garden with a large wooden deck, built-in pizza oven and huge gas barbecue. Lewis's eyes widened. 'Ah, you got it? Lucky man. Yes, tasty.'

Brin preened in the sunshine. 'Back home in Ireland it's always hit and miss for barbecue weather. But here, it's pretty much always a hit. Thought I'd get the best one I could.'

Lewis lovingly ran his fingers over the chrome and cooed the way he had at Stella. 'She's a beauty. I have serious barbecue envy.'

'Men!' Laughing, Charlie looked round the little crowd of people for some female cavalry and noted Mia walking towards her. 'Hello. Thank goodness you're here. I was starting feel pressured into have a conversation about the benefits of gas barbecues over charcoal and boast about how many burners mine has.' Charlie puffed out her chest and flexed her left bicep.

'Men! Good to see you again, Charlie.' Mia laughed and gave her a hug. 'Let's leave them to their barbecue adoration. My daughter's around here somewhere. She's so excited to be having a party. And who is this?' She stroked Stella's hand.

'This is my niece, Stella. We left Mum relaxing in the bath at home. She needed some time off.'

Mia raised her eyebrows and groaned in delight. 'Oh, lucky lady.'

'Yes.' *Not lucky at all.* 'I was wondering if it would be okay to put Stella down for a nap somewhere in about an hour or so?'

'No problem at all. We've got a travel cot. I can put that up in Harper's room and she can nap in there.'

'I don't want to put you to any trouble.'

'Not at all. There are a few babies and kids coming, so it'll be put to good use.' Mia glanced at the kitchen door and smiled at a couple walking into the garden. 'Excuse me while I go welcome my other guests. I'll be back in a minute. Help yourself to a drink.' Mia pointed to a table with glasses and a large cool box filled with ice, bottles of wine, beer and soft drinks.

'Yes. Sure.' Although, she wasn't sure how she was going to manage that with a baby in her arms. She'd have to wait until Lewis came to her rescue. Her heart crumpled a little. Her knight in shining armour had always been exactly that. Too much. Too long ago.

She didn't have to wait long. While Lewis turned sausages on the barbecue, Brin brought her a glass of wine then steered her towards the newly arrived couple standing with Mia. He introduced her to Carly and Owen, who lived on Rāwhiti Island, and their boy Mason. Owen shook her hand. 'Your name's familiar. Maybe our paths have crossed?'

'I'm working in A and E at Auckland Central at the moment. Emergency registrar.'

'Ah. That must be it. I've probably had a discharge letter from you for some of my patients.' It turned out that Owen was a doctor too. He used to have a practice in the city but now worked full-time on the island. Charlie remembered that Mia was a practice nurse working for a GP partnership just up the road.

'Is there anyone here who isn't a medic?' Charlie laughed, then lost her breath as she saw Lewis heading over towards them. His smile was so warm and friendly, and she thought back to the days when they used to host parties like this. When he'd casually wrap his arm around her waist as they chatted, just the way Brin was doing to Mia now.

Lewis kissed Carly and shook hands with Owen. It seemed they all knew each other very well, leaving Charlie feeling just a little out of the loop.

Owen stood back and looked Lewis up and down. 'Hey, looking sharp, man.'

'All that training,' Brin quipped.

'Oh? Training for what?' Charlie asked. Lewis

hadn't mentioned any training or event, although they had been distracted by other things recently: making love, navigating a fledgling friendship and kissing, mostly.

Her core heated at that thought and she drew her gaze from his sharp-looking body and made faces to entertain Stella, who was getting heavy and restless on her hip.

Brin put his hand on Lewis's shoulder and spoke in an extremely proud fatherly tone. 'This guy is a machine. We did the vertical challenge as a work team and you should have seen him go.'

'What's a vertical challenge?' Charlie asked. 'Sounds painful.'

'Running up fifty-one levels of the Sky Tower, and he left us all for dust. Which was pretty favourable, as it happens, because it meant we made a mint for charity too. He's a bona-fide legend.' Brin's eyes flitted to Charlie and she got the distinct impression he was saying all of this for her benefit.

But, yes, he was indeed a legend. Because not only was he super-fit for work but he used his skills, strength, spare energy and even money to support charities: first the silent auction, now the vertical challenge. *Impressive.*

But then, she knew that already. She caught Lewis's eye and he shook his head, clearly embarrassed at all the praise, but laughing. His gaze locked on hers and he rolled his eyes, as if to say, *this guy, huh?*

It was time to put poor Brin to rights, for the truth to be told at last. She cleared her throat. 'Yes, Lewis has always been devoted to being fit for his job—running, gym work, swimming. I used to call him an exercise junkie.'

Brin frowned and glanced from Lewis to Charlie. '*Always*? How do you…? Did you two know each other before you started working together?'

'You could say that.' She licked her lips and glanced at Lewis to make sure it was okay for her to explain their relationship. He nodded and smiled encouragingly. 'We were married once.'

'What?' Brin's expression turned from interest to shock to a full-on blush. He smacked his forehead with his palm. 'Here I was pushing you two together, thinking you both needed…company.' He coughed. 'I am so sorry.'

'Don't worry. It's okay, honestly.' She looked directly at Lewis and her tummy tumbled in delight and confusion. 'We're friends now.'

'Right. Wow, okay. Well, friends is good at least. Because that could have made for a mighty awkward barbecue otherwise.' Brin inhaled, then turned to Lewis, bugging his eyes at his friend. 'And you were going to tell me when, *partner*?'

'Now seemed like a good time.' Lewis laughed. 'I'm sorry to let you find out this way but you did kind of deserve it.'

'Jeez, mate. I am mortified.' Brin shook his head, but chuckled. '*Mortified.*'

'It'll wear off. Have another beer. Seriously, we're good, aren't we, Charlie?' Lewis looked over at Charlie and his laugh died away as his gaze settled on Stella wriggling. 'Whoa, little one, fancy giving your auntie a break? She's got a sore shoulder and you're probably not helping.'

'Thanks.' Charlie eased out the muscles in her neck as she passed the baby over to him to hold. 'She's getting a bit grizzly.'

He frowned at Stella, as if trying to solve a maths equation. 'Something to eat, maybe?'

'It's not long since she had a snack but we could try another one, I guess.'

He jiggled Stella up and down on his hip, blowing raspberries at her in a vain attempt to make the little girl laugh, to no avail. He grimaced. 'Raspberries usually work with my girls. Maybe she's tired?'

My girls. Her heart melted as he referenced Lily, Lola and Luna. 'Maybe. Mia said I could put her down in Harper's room.'

Lewis nodded. 'Great idea. You take her up and I'll grab her changing bag from the kitchen. We can give her some milk and see if it helps her drop off?'

So they really were the dream team now. 'Sure. Yes, thanks. The powder's in a little pot and you need to heat—'

'The milk carefully. And test the temperature on the back of my hand. I know.' He winked. 'I've got this. Go.'

Oh, Lewis. Her throat was suddenly raw and scratchy. She felt dejected that she couldn't give him the gift of fatherhood that he craved and was perfect for, yet her heart lifted to have him want to share this with her. She was a good auntie and would always hold Stella very close to her heart. She blinked back the stab of tears as she took Stella from him, feeling his heat and strength as he passed the baby over. Then she walked upstairs on wobbly legs, trying to put her attraction and sadness into a metaphorical box and leave it there.

She'd thought she'd got over the sadness years ago. And she could generally deal with it if it raised its head. She'd had therapy; she knew there was no surmounting the facts of her body's limits. There was no point in wishing for impossible things.

But it was the attraction that continually derailed her. She wanted him in so many ways.

And it was dangerous, making her reckless.

Making her forget all her promises to keep away.

CHAPTER THIRTEEN

LEWIS CAREFULLY OPENED the door into the dimly lit bedroom, and then paused, rooted to the spot.

Charlie was sitting in a nursing chair, cradling Stella and singing softly, a nursery lullaby. She was stroking the baby's head, staring lovingly down at her, while Stella's little fist bumped against Charlie's arm as she grizzled and fussed.

His chest hurt at the sight. Charlie was beautiful, that was all, stunning. And he hated that she would never get to hold her own child. He swallowed and tried to clear the lump in his throat.

'Hey,' he whispered, stepping into the room and closing the door against the loud, happy chatter of the party downstairs. 'Here's her bottle.'

'Thanks.' She looked up at him and smiled, taking the warm bottle and offering it to Stella. The baby immediately started to suck greedily. 'Oh, you were hungry, weren't you? I can't keep up with you.'

He watched Stella's breathless sucks. 'Yep, that definitely seems to be the answer.'

'I can't believe how much this baby eats.' She

laughed. 'Hey, go down and talk to your friends. You don't have to stay here with me.'

Leaving them both here would be a wise thing to do, but he couldn't tear himself away. This was so intimate, so exactly what they'd dreamt about. It was too lovely to leave. He would just indulge himself for a few minutes and play that game of 'what if?'; what might have been; pretend they didn't have a million obstacles from their past pressing in on them. Just a few more moments.

'It's okay. I'll wait. You might need something else. How about a glass of wine? A plate of food?'

'No need. I'm fine, thanks.' She glanced at Stella and then back at him with an adorable smile. 'I think we've managed to get her off.'

'Sometimes it's the simplest of things, right? Peace and quiet and a full belly. That certainly works for me.'

'I remember. My mum used to say she'd never met anyone who ate as much as you did.' Charlie laughed. She was looking at him so fondly, the tension of the last few days gone from her face. The tension of their last two heart-breaking years together completely erased. She looked young and bright and ethereal in the orange glow from the night light.

He decided to focus on Stella because there was no good in doing or thinking anything else. And because the obstacles of the present threatened now too. 'There were a lot of new faces for her to take in down there; she might have been a bit overwhelmed.' He bent in front of Charlie and the milk-drunk baby. 'You want me to pop her in the cot?'

'Thanks. Yes. She's little but she's getting heavier every day.'

He slid his hands under the sleeping babe, very gently deposited her onto the cot mattress and covered her with a blanket. This whole scenario felt surreal: the warmth; the baby; Charlie. It was *cosy*.

He turned back to look at her. 'Are you ready to go back down?'

She wrinkled her nose and shook her head. 'Not quite.'

He sighed. 'I get it. Sometimes all those new faces are overwhelming for adults too. I'm sorry you don't know many people here.'

'It's fine. I want to make friends and all yours seem lovely. I just need a minute to catch my breath.' She giggled softly. 'Oh, my God, did you see poor Brin's face? I felt bad that I told him about our connection like that.'

'Poor Brin nothing.' Lewis chuckled. Making sure Stella was fast asleep and their voices wouldn't wake her, he slid down the wall and sat on the floor next to Charlie's chair. 'He's been trying to get us together since he set eyes on you. For some reason he seems to think we're a good fit.'

'For *some* reason?' She laughed hollowly.

'Maybe he sees us the way we used to see each other?'

Oh, the delicious, poignant naivety of youth. No one had ever been in love as much as they had. No one could possibly have known how it felt to be them, falling deeper and deeper, as if they'd been unbeatable for ever. He smiled at the memories bombarding his brain. 'I liked those days, back when we were starting out—dating, our wedding day...'

'Yes. Good times.' Her tone was as wistful as he felt. 'You remember when we were in sixth form and just started seeing each other, how I used to sneak out from home in the middle of the night and climb through your bedroom window?' She laughed. 'Good job you had a bungalow.'

'And when your parents found out and grounded you, I sneaked into your bedroom instead...via a tree-climb and a drain pipe. Almost broke my neck on more than two occasions.'

'We didn't care. It added to the drama of our...' She put her hand to her chest and swayed softly from side to side, then whispered, almost as if she couldn't bring herself to say the word, 'Love'.

Love that had shattered under pressure. He tried for a lighter note. 'You remember when Uncle Paul tripped and almost fell onto our uncut wedding cake?'

'And we all held our breath when his hand flew out as he careened towards the table. Luckily he righted himself before disaster struck.' She laughed. 'And Logan's best man speech. He was so funny.'

Lewis tutted at the memory of his brother spilling too many of Lewis's boyhood antics. 'I could have killed him at times.'

'Oh, everyone thought it was hilarious. Then all the bridesmaids did a flash-mob dance and you...*you* knew all about it and never told me.' She nudged his leg with hers. 'We had the best wedding, Lewis.'

He felt the punch of pride now in his solar plexus as much as he had that day so long ago. The first time he'd seen her as she'd stepped into the little church, the sun haloing her from behind, had taken his breath away. 'I felt like I was the luckiest damned man in the world. I couldn't believe you'd chosen me.'

'Oh, Lewis. I was the lucky one.' Her hand slid down by the side of the chair next to him and he couldn't stop himself from taking her palm and stroking it. Then he slipped his fingers between hers. He heard her breathing hitch, felt a shift in the atmosphere, but she didn't let go.

They sat for a few minutes in silence. He listened to Stella's even breaths and his more staccato ones. He wondered what was going on in Charlie's head.

Then she inhaled and said, 'Lewis, can I ask you something?'

He dared not hope or think what it might be. 'Sure.'

'If it wasn't for me having to look after Lucy would you want a rerun of the other night?'

Yes. God, yes.

'If things weren't complicated? If we had no past? If we'd just met, two strangers?' Maybe here in the dark they could be honest about the way they felt because, in the real world, they couldn't admit that these feelings were growing.

She squeezed his hand. 'Or if none of the bad stuff had happened. Yes.'

'Then, yes. I wouldn't just want a rerun, I'd want more, Charlie.'

'Oh, God.' Silence lingered for a beat, then two. Then she breathed out. 'Me too.'

The baby stirred, a little cry that had him glancing over to the cot. He held his breath, wondering if he needed to go to her, but she seemed to settle on her own. His gaze drifted to a little device above the bed. 'Damn. Check the monitor—make sure it's not on.' The last thing they needed was an audience downstairs listening to their intimate confessions.

'I can't see a light on. We're good.' Charlie sighed and paused. 'Lewis…'

'Yes?'

There came another pause, then, 'The harder I try to keep away from you, the more I struggle.'

'*Charlie*. Please.' He closed his eyes and tried to

control his stuttered exhale. It was too much; too much for him to handle. His heart hammered and his chest felt hollowed out. Because what did 'what if?' matter if they couldn't act on it? Being honest was a mistake. Staying up here was a mistake.

And yet he wanted it. He wanted her, wanted it all, so much that it was a physical ache he could not erase.

He was at risk here—serious risk. He'd tried so hard to make things work before, and then had watched her walk away, and it had left him broken. He couldn't let her do it again, no matter how much he wanted her. So he slipped his fingers out from hers. 'Okay. Well, I'd better go see if Brin needs help with the barbecue.'

Then he forced himself to stand up and walk away.

Because, if he didn't leave right then, he would something they both might regret.

'This is baby Leo Hudson. Eight months old.' Lewis's voice sounded uncharacteristically strained as he lifted the fitting baby onto the trolley in the resus room. Sick babies did that to Charlie too. It didn't matter how long she'd been doing this job, or how many kids she treated, poorly babies tugged hard at every thread of maternal instinct she had.

She looked up into Lewis's eyes and her heart ached and jumped. She had an intense urge to reach for him and soothe away the pain in his eyes, but she refused to allow herself to be derailed from this emergency. This little one needed all their focus so they could fit the diagnosis jigsaw puzzle together. She nodded for him to continue.

'No medical history of note. Normal vaginal delivery at thirty-nine weeks. Generally well, but has been grizzly and snotty the last couple of days. Parents reported seeing some unusual twitching and jerking that has not stopped for a good hour and has worsened. No history of epilepsy or previous seizures. Airway is patent, oxygen administered, blood glucose normal. Temperature a little high at thirty-eight point one. IO Midazolam administered en route with no effect. Mum's just outside. Dad's followed in the car with two older children.'

'Thanks, Lewis. Arno,' she called to one of the senior nurses. 'Page Paeds, please—*urgently*. Tell them we have a status epilepticus. Someone please go talk to Mum and explain that we're doing all we can and I'll come talk to her when I get a chance.'

'I've explained some,' Lewis said. 'I'll go have a word in a minute. She said she'd wait in reception until her husband got here, but she's frantic with worry.'

'Understandable. Thanks. Take one of the nurses too; they'll be able to bring her in to see Leo once we've got him stable.' She knew Lewis would have built some rapport when he had attended the emergency. *Eight months old*—not much older than Stella. She could only imagine the way the mum was feeling, but she'd be in good hands with Lewis.

She grabbed the tiny oxygen mask and held it over the baby's mouth while she started her assessment. 'He's tachycardic with poor peripheral perfusion, pupils unreactive. Can I have a temperature reading please? And let's try another bolus of Midazolam.'

She was aware of Lewis's presence as they worked on the infant. By some miracle in the back of a moving ambulance, he'd managed to get IV access into Leo's tiny veins. He'd explained everything to the little baby, even though Leo wouldn't have a clue what was happening. It was comforting to have an extra pair of hands helping.

Then suddenly he wasn't there any more and she missed his strength and solid steadiness next to her. Was it her imagination that he was avoiding her? Every time he'd been in the department recently he'd barely glanced her way. Sure, he'd done his job professionally and efficiently, just as he was doing now, but there was no friendly chit chat afterwards. Maybe the closeness they'd shared on Saturday night had scared him away. Maybe she was over-thinking, and being a tad too sensitive. He was a busy man after all, and why would he specifically choose to chat to her at work?

Or maybe she was falling harder and quicker than she'd thought. Because, it had been six days since their heart-to-heart in Harper's bedroom and she'd burned every moment since just to see him again.

After she'd handed over to the paediatrics team, she stepped outside to get a breath of fresh air. From the back door of the emergency department she could see the hospital nursery and felt a pull to go and see Stella. Lately she'd been spending quite a lot of her break time with her niece and she realised it wasn't just to keep Stella happy: it fed something inside Charlie too.

She saw Seung walk by and called over, 'Hey, I'm well past due my break. Just popping over to the nursery. I'll be back soon as.'

'No worries.' Seung waved. 'Paeds are sorting Leo out. Arno's with Mum and Dad, and they're having a cup of tea before they all go up to Peter Pan Ward. Everywhere else is quiet.'

'Hush! Do not say that. Don't! You'll jinx us.' She waved back and headed across the car park for some serious snuggles with her favourite six-month-old.

But it wasn't Stella or Leo on her mind right now. It was Lewis. It felt as if she would never get used to working with him. Ever since the barbecue, all her shifts since had coincided with his. Which meant she couldn't get away from her admission in that darkened room: she was struggling to keep away from him and, in an ideal world, she'd want more and take more.

And she would never forget the tender stroke of his hand, the way she'd wanted to sink into another kiss with him or the deep yearning she had to be in his arms, in his bed, in his life.

Yes, back in his life, which would be a one-way ticket to heartbreak.

She'd been both glad and sad when he'd gone back down to the party, because she'd been feeling so mixed up she hadn't known what to do. So she'd stayed upstairs for as long as she could without appearing impolite to her hosts, until Mia had come looking for her and coaxed her down for some food. Of course, somehow she'd ended up sitting next to Lewis, and the rest of the evening had been pure torture.

Every time she'd looked round, he'd been there with his smile, his dark eyes glittering. She'd caught his scent on the air and felt the whisper of his breath as he laughed. And with every second she spent with him the torture had intensified. They both knew the truth of their need but she knew they could not, would not, *should not* act on it—not again.

It had almost been a relief for him to drop her home, her hands mercifully too full of baby and bags to reach for him and tug him close. A relief to close the door behind her and be free of his tempting presence. Yet here he was, every day in her space, at her place of work, tempting and torturing her. And, of course, there he was now, in her direct path, putting something into the boot of his car.

She closed her eyes and took a moment to erase any giveaway facial expressions, trying to act normally instead of jumping into his arms. 'Hey, Lewis.'

'Hey. Finished up for the day?' He was standing right where they'd had their first 'this time round' kiss. Her body flushed at the memory. Since then they'd vowed not to get involved and yet had shared a wonderful night together. They'd admitted feelings for each other, but agreed they couldn't act on them again.

No wonder she was confused.

She found him a smile. 'Not yet. I've got another couple of hours to go. Just going to see Stella in my break time. I feel a need to hug her.' She didn't want to admit to the rest of her work colleagues that she'd been shaken up dealing with a sick baby, but she knew Lewis would understand.

'Yep, I get that. Sometimes a hug works wonders.' He nodded. 'How's the little lad doing?'

It seemed she didn't even need to explain why she had the urge to see her niece. 'We managed to stop the fitting. He's on his way up to the ward now and stabilised, but it'll be a while until we know what's causing the seizures.'

He stepped closer, his expression concerned. 'You okay, though?'

'Yep.' She blew out a breath. 'You know how it is, sick kids are hard to deal with sometimes.'

'Yeah. I dread the day I get a call out for Lola, Lily or Luna.'

She shuddered. 'Here's hoping that will never happen.'

'Indeed. It was bad enough that I had to attend your accident. It's always worse when you know the person involved.'

She hadn't actually given any thought to how he must have felt seeing her potentially injured, only to how he'd felt seeing her in the flesh again. 'Well, I for one am very glad it was you.'

'Don't you dare do that to me again.' He gave her a rueful smile.

'I'll try not to. Once is enough.' Then she remembered something that would make his smile grow. 'Oh, I had a call from the High Dependency Unit this morning. Graham's been transferred out of ICU and has been asking to see us.'

'Really?' It was lovely to see the genuine and huge smile bloom on his face, all trace of worry defused. 'I never get to see patients once they're out of my hands.'

'I was thinking about popping up there after my shift ends. Maybe we could go together?' It made sense, didn't it?

But his expression clouded. 'Oh. I don't know...'

'We're going to see a patient, Lewis. I'm not

going to...' *Oh, hell. How to broach this?* 'Not going to say more of the things I said on Saturday.'

'Oh. Right.' He breathed out, looking a little taken aback and also relieved. 'No, me neither. I guess I could come with you. I'm off for the next couple of days so it would save me coming back into town to visit him. And, to be honest, I do really want to see the guy that survived CPR in the pouring rain.'

Flash-flooding florecast.

'Me too.' Grinning at the memory of what they'd done after saving Graham's life, she checked the time. 'Say, two and a half hours?'

'Sure. I've got paperwork to catch up on anyway so I could do that until you're ready.' He slammed the boot closed. 'I'll meet you outside HDU.'

Despite everything she'd promised herself, her tummy tumbled at the thought of seeing him again so soon. 'Can't wait.'

'Me neither. It'll be good to see him. Enjoy the Stella hugs. Say hi from me. See you soon, Charlie.' He turned and flashed her a look that was filled with the kind of promise that had her knees turning to jelly.

It's not a date, silly woman. He couldn't wait to see Graham, not to see her.

It was the way things were going to be. Had to be—two colleagues doing colleague-type things. Friends doing friend-type things. Because, upstairs at Brin's in that little dark room, she'd found the courage to tell him what she wanted and he'd let go of her hand and walked away, telling her through his actions that he was still too bruised, or hurt, to try again. Or that he was protecting himself...*from her*...and that thought made her heart hurt.

But it didn't stop the wish for the hugs she so badly needed to come from him. Or the senseless hope for the promise of more.

Because she couldn't ignore it any longer: she wanted more. Wanted more chats about their day and the shared patients they saw; more time with him; more kisses, more hugs; more *everything* with Lewis.

And that was going to be her downfall.

CHAPTER FOURTEEN

HIS HEART TRIPPED as he found Charlotte outside HDU. She'd changed out of her scrubs into a pretty pale-pink summer dress and white cardigan. Her hair hung loosely around her shoulders. *God,* he loved her hair. And she was carrying chocolates he recognised from the hospital shop in the lobby downstairs. It was so sweet she'd had the fore-thought to do that.

She beamed at him, excitement clear in her ex-pression. 'Hey, Lewis.'

'Hey.' His immediate instinct was to reach out his hand for her to hold but he reined it in. So far, since Saturday, his avoidance tactics had been working. The less time he spent with her, the better. But, the moment she'd invited him to see the guy they'd worked on together, he'd folded. He knew he'd have folded at some time. He just couldn't keep away from her. It seemed as though she was a magnetic force he was destined to spin around.

He gestured to the door. 'Should we?'

'Indeed.' Her smile was infectious.

He buzzed the intercom and they were let in

by the ward clerk, who showed them to Graham's bed. He was sitting upright, propped up by pillows. His arm was in a sling, his bruised chest dotted with sticky heart-monitor pads and he had a nasal cannula taped to his cheek delivering oxygen. His frail-looking features lit up as they approached and he raised his good arm in a small wave.

'Graham, hello.' Lewis gently shook the man's hand. 'I'm Lewis and this is Charlie. We're the paramedic and doctor who just happened to be in the right place at the right time a couple of weeks ago. Well, you're certainly looking better than the last time we met.'

'I hope so.' Graham's voice was weak even though he was clearly on the mend. 'Sorry if I don't recognise you, but I can't remember much of it.'

Lewis smiled. 'That's absolutely fine. You were a bit out of it.'

Understatement of the year.

Charlie sat down next to the bed. 'It was a hell of a night. All that rain didn't help. But we're so glad to see that you're out of the woods. Hope you feel up to eating these soon.' She handed Graham the box of chocolates.

'Thank you. I hope so too.' Graham nodded. He looked first at Charlie and then at Lewis, as if committing them to memory. 'They tell me that you two saved my life.'

Lewis glanced over at Charlie. 'Well, we did our best to keep your heart going until we could hand you over to the team. You're obviously one hell of a fighter, Graham.'

'You need to be these days. But I'm glad you two were on my side.' He laughed, which brought on a coughing fit. His monitor started to beep and a nurse came running over. She tutted and frowned, but her tone was jolly. 'Graham, honestly. What do I keep telling you about overdoing things?'

'I'm fine. I'm fine.' He waved her away weakly then looked at Charlie. 'I want you to know how much I appreciate what you both did. I owe you my life.'

'It's our pleasure. We were lucky to be there to help.' She smiled at him and patted his hand. 'Now, we don't want to put you under any more stress or tire you out, so we'll say good bye for now. We'll pop back again soon and, in the meantime, keep getting better, Graham.'

The old man smiled and nodded, exhaustion bruising his eyes. 'What a lovely couple you are. Thank you again.'

Couple. It seemed as though everyone thought they should be or could be a couple...except the couple themselves.

Lewis glanced at Charlie. Her cheeks bloomed red, which was interesting, because she'd handled telling Brin the truth about their relationship so easily the other day. She scrunched up her nose as she smiled. 'Just doing our jobs. Get well soon, Graham.'

Lewis's heart felt lighter as they walked out of the ward and Charlie's smile was wide, her eyes dancing with light as she said, 'That was lovely.'

'Always great to meet a success story,' he agreed. But it was the happy glow in Charlie's eyes that was making his heart thump more quickly, not pride in doing his job well. She looked almost ethereal in that flowing dress. All he wanted to do was capture her mouth and taste that smile.

They wandered through the hospital and out into the car park, chatting about success stories and the weird and unusual cases they'd seen. So far, so collegial.

But once out in the car park she stopped, her expression morphing from animated to cautious. 'Lewis?'

His heart started to hammer against his chest. Where was this going? 'Yes?'

'Look, I just want you to know that you don't have to avoid me at work.'

'What do you mean?' He knew exactly what she meant.

She looked stricken. 'It just feels as if every time we meet on the department, you're very keen to make a quick retreat from my presence.'

Damn right he was keen not to spend any time with her. It was self-preservation, really. The more time he spent with her, the more torture it became. He *wanted* her…always. 'No. That's not it, Charlie…'

'Okay, maybe I'm being sensitive then. Sorry, forget I mentioned it. It's just… Oh, look, never mind.' Her brightness and elation of a few minutes ago now flattened, she turned away.

Now he felt as if he was gaslighting her, just because he wanted to protect his own heart from further damage, and he couldn't do that. He reached out and touched her shoulder. 'Wait, Charlie. I'm sorry. You're right: I have been trying to spend less time in the emergency department, if I can.'

'Oh?' She turned back to him, looking hurt. 'Because of me?'

Ugh. He'd been trying to be honest with her as much as he could. She kept asking him, pushing him to tell her how he was feeling, and she was showing him how, so why couldn't he do it?

He took a breath. 'Um…okay. So, what we said on Saturday… It's been playing on my mind— occupying it, actually.' He smiled but he knew it had a hint of wariness in it. 'I'm confused, if I'm honest. You coming back has thrown me for six. I need some space to get my head round everything. More for my benefit than yours.'

Her frown deepened. 'That makes me feel so many things, Lewis. I'm upset that you feel you have to actively avoid me and I'm so…so sad we can't be friends. Especially after what we said on

Saturday.' She swallowed, her eyes large and soft. 'I thought I was doing okay, you know? But, the truth is, I'm not okay. I miss the closeness we once had. Sometimes, I just want to talk to you.'

As with today; after attending to a sick baby, she'd needed a hug and had had to get it from her niece, not from him.

'Oh, Charlie.' His heart felt as if it were turning inside out. He hated to see her upset, and because of something he'd done. Before he could stop himself, he'd pulled her into his arms. He stroked her hair as she lent her head against his chest. 'I'm here for you. Talk to me any time you want.'

She looked up at him and smiled almost shyly. Then she turned her head away, holding him tight, hugging him to her. As they stood there in that desolate car park, he felt the rise and fall of her chest and heard the soft sound of her breath. Awareness prickled through him. Something changed in the atmosphere around them, like a buzz of electricity sparking through him. His skin tingled at each pressure point where his body touched hers.

Her head nuzzled against his chin. He closed his eyes, trying to force away the urge to kiss her again, trying to wish away the growing erection between them. But she made a little sound in her throat and in the next moment all his fight was snapped into a thousand pieces, leaving just desire and heat winding through him.

'Sometimes I want more, Lewis. Sometimes

I don't want to talk at all.' Her mouth was close to his ear, her warm breath tickling his skin. He turned his face to hers and she was so close, so very close. 'Just touch. And… I know that's not fair, because I can't give you what you want…the family you want.'

Right now, *she* was all he wanted. All he'd ever wanted. Her pupils were huge and her breathing fast. Her eyelids fluttered closed as her fingers stroked his back. Her hot body pressed against him in all the right places, her breasts against his chest, her core against his growing erection.

Then he couldn't control anything any longer. He walked her back towards his car and pressed her against it, capturing her mouth in his. 'Charlie. God, Charlie…'

Next he was kissing, kissing and kissing her, telling her in his kisses exactly what he wanted: that he couldn't bear to see her confused or upset; that he couldn't keep holding back; that he'd rather die than not be able to slide inside her, to hold her, to drown in her kisses.

'I had to avoid you because all I want to do is this.' He dragged his lips from hers, framing her face with his palms. 'You are the only woman I've ever wanted, Charlie. My Charlie Rose.'

He kissed her again, long, slowly and sensuously, and she whimpered…or was it him?

'I love the way you kiss me. I love…' She suddenly pulled back, shaking and breathless. 'Shoot. I...um... I have to go pick up Stella from nursery.'

I love... You...? Was that what she'd been about to say?

No. No. No. That was not where they were heading. He couldn't allow it full-stop. She'd loved him last time, but not enough to stay. Not enough to try and make things work. She loved his kisses, that was all.

'Yeah. I should go too.' His voice was gravelly as reality hit him hard. Firstly, they were kissing in the staff car park where anyone could see them. And secondly, and far more importantly, they'd stepped right over that line again. Blurred everything into a kiss, into hot need, into something from which he didn't know he could disentangle himself.

She swallowed, her hand on her chest as if trying to calm down her racing heart. 'And I need to check on Lucy too. She had another dose of chemo last week, so this week is where she starts to feel yuck again.'

'Of course. Of course.' He watched her walk away, feeling the pull to walk with her, to stay by her side. To talk whenever she needed him to, to listen, to soothe and to kiss.

But he couldn't ask where this was going or what this blurring of boundaries might mean. Couldn't put her in that situation to make rational choices when she was so involved with caring for her family. And he had no idea himself what could happen next, only that with every new moment spent with her…every kiss, every touch and with every *I love*…he was drawn back under her spell.

And he didn't know if he could fight it any more. Even though he had to, if he was going to get out sane.

She tried to keep away. She spent about thirty-two solid hours tending to Lucy's and Stella's every need when she wasn't at work. She focused on helping them get through this difficult week and tried to put Lewis to the back of her mind.

It was a futile exercise, of course. Because when she wasn't holding Lucy's hair back as she vomited, or changing Stella's nappy, cooing her to sleep, cajoling her to eat or reading her a picture book, the only thing she thought about was Lewis.

She still wanted him.

She wanted him right now, standing outside his house, wondering if she had actually gone mad with need, desire or…whatever it was that she refused to put a name to. Because if she acknowledged the depth of her feelings she'd have to walk away. So she told herself it was lust and possibly loneliness. That both those things could be easily remedied by sex, by friendship, maybe a combination of the two.

Friends with benefits—would he agree to that?

She pressed the doorbell and heard the echoing

ring inside. She waited. Her heart thudded as she craned to hear thumping footsteps.

Nothing.

She pressed the bell again and waited. Maybe he wasn't here after all. Maybe he was fast asleep and couldn't hear the bell. Maybe he knew it was her and was choosing to ignore her, like a sensible person, not lust-drunk, would.

Eventually she turned away and started to walk down the path.

'Charlie?'

She whipped round, her breath stalling in her chest as the sight of him, in an old grey T-shirt and tight black boxer shorts made her feel dizzy with need. Could he look any sexier?

'Charlie?' His face crumpled as he reached out his hand, immediately worried. 'What's wrong?'

Her courage started to fail her. But she had to say something. 'Can I come in?'

'Sure.' He opened the door wider and let her walk in front of him into his lounge, switching on the wall lights, bringing a warm, soft glow. 'What's happened? Is everything all right?'

She turned to look at him, her heart pounding in her ears. 'Everything is fine. Don't worry.'

'Is Lucy okay? Stella?'

'Yes.' She smiled at his concern. 'Calm down, Lewis. They're fine. They're fast asleep.'

He shook his head. 'So, why are you here?'

Such a bad idea after all. She sighed and chuckled. 'It never used to be this difficult. For God's sake, do I have to spell it out? This is the adult woman version of sneaking out of my house in the middle of the night.'

He gasped, then laughed…more of a groan. 'Charlie Jade Rose—this is a booty call? What the hell?'

'What can I say? I wanted to see you. I couldn't sleep and wondered if you couldn't either.'

'As it happens, I was wide awake.' He met her gaze, suddenly heated. 'Thinking about you, actually.'

Thinking about what, exactly? 'You took your time answering the door.'

He ran his hand through his hair, eyes wide. 'I didn't think for a minute that it could be you. I thought it was kids messing about.'

She took a breath, thinking about what they used to get up to in his bedroom, in *their* bedroom, back when things had been fun. 'Maybe we could be.'

He swallowed and grinned. Clearly he remembered too. 'Charlie…' His voice was guttural, base.

It was probably meant to be a warning. A reminder of everything they'd agreed. But it sounded like the sexiest growl she'd ever heard.

'So, tell me to go if you're not…up for it…' She stepped towards him, or he stepped towards her; she wasn't sure. But suddenly he was up close, his forehead against hers, his hand snaking round her waist.

'How did you know my address?'

'Is it very lame to say I remembered from way back when we were checking to see if we were neighbours?' She chuckled. 'Plus, your car is parked in the drive.'

'Ah.' He nodded, swallowing hard as he looked her up and down, his gaze landing on her mouth. 'Doesn't take a genius, then.'

'And you're worrying about details and I'm standing here wanting you. Does my seduction technique need work?' She raised her eyebrows in question as she snaked her arms around his waist. 'It never used to fail me. You used to welcome me with a kiss and take me straight to bed.'

The cloud of hesitation that seemed to have been hovering over him dissipated. He laughed, his fingers trailing over her cheek. 'You have a seduction technique?'

'Hey, you.' She giggled. 'I can seduce.'

'Really? Interesting. Tell me when you're starting.' Tongue in cheek, he grinned, pretending to be immune to her advances when the tent in his boxer shorts told her he very much wasn't immune at all.

But he did have a point: she actually had to do or say something. Shrugging off her coat, she revealed her matching black lace bra and panties. God, she'd taken such a risk coming here in the middle of the night dressed like this. But it could be worth every threaded breath, every second-guess, every kiss, every touch, every stroke of his fingertips against her skin. Every second spent in his arms. 'You're telling me you hadn't thought about Sunday morning sex?'

'It's still...' His eyes darted to the wall clock. 'Oh, wait. Yes, Sunday morning. *Charlie...*'

Then his mouth found hers in a greedy, desperate kiss. He palmed her breast and she reached for his pants, each of them stripping each other in a haze of clumsy, desperate hunger.

Still kissing her as if he never wanted to let go, he tugged her to the bedroom and laid her on the bed. She reached for him, stroking her fingers down his length. He was so hard....for her.

After this, she would go.

Sunday morning sex—just sex. Just friends and sex, and that was all.

She swallowed back the rawness in her throat. Whatever label they put on it, it was hot and irresistible. She put aside their promises, ignoring the beat of anxiety at the back of her mind, and sank into this, with him—with Lewis.

He shuddered at her touch and groaned again. 'Jeez, Charlie. What you do to me...'

She whispered into his ear, 'Is what?'

'You turn me on so much.'

'Aha.' She slicked kisses across his throat. 'How?'

'You're supposed to be seducing me, right? Not the other way round.' He laughed and whispered, 'What do you want, Charlotte?'

'Oh, it's Charlotte now?' She laughed, then the laughter died in her throat as she thought about what she wanted.

I want you to hold me, to hug me. To be with me. I want you inside me. I want you to... I want you, Lewis. I want you, so much I can't breathe.

'I want to kiss you, Lewis. I want you to fill me. I want to ride you.'

'Jeez...' His breath stuttered on the inhale.

'Do you want that too?' She kissed his jaw, his bottom lip and his top lip, stroking him gently up and down, up and down... 'Tell me what you want.'

'I want to slide deep inside you. I want to feel you around me.' He turned onto his side and slid his hand between her legs, arrowing for her core and rubbing the sensitive spot right...*there*.

He stroked her, then slid his fingers inside her, making her squirm, contract and writhe against him. He was telling her what he needed. *Hell...* Sex had always been great with Lewis, but he'd never actually told her what he wanted. They'd just gone by feel and instinct before. It had been enough back then. She'd loved the way they'd made love. But this was next-level sexy. She was breathing so fast, she could barely get enough air into her lungs.

Her grip on him tightened and he groaned in delight. She was so dizzy with need she could barely form words. 'I want…'

'What else do you want, Charlie?'

'Everything.' She wanted this, wanted him. Wanted what they'd had years ago, before it had all gone wrong. Wanted this new thing they had going, this honesty, this need.

She'd only ever wanted him.

He lay back and lifted her onto his lap. '*God*, Charlie. I need to be inside you.'

Hot, electric need coursed through her and she knew she was hanging on the edge. One move, one thrust of him inside her, and she'd be undone.

'Now. Please. *Now.*' She straddled his thighs, his erection hard against her core. She positioned herself over him and lowered herself with a moan. And he was inside her again, rocking slowly, and it was so intense and perfect; perfectly intense.

She closed her eyes as their rhythm quickened, catching her breath in stuttered gasps. The pressure rising at her core sent flashes of sparks and light flickering across her skin, over her, inside her, deep and white-hot. She felt him ripple, heard him grind out her name and she clung on and rode with him until they were both crying out, mouths welded together in a messy, needy, hungry kiss.

Together. First and last.

Her Lewis. Her love. Her always.

CHAPTER FIFTEEN

IT TOOK SOME time for her breathing to steady and for her to feel emotionally anchored enough to climb off his thighs and snuggle against him. He wrapped his arms around her, hugging her the way she needed. If she was honest, that was what she'd come for, after all. Making love had been an accumulation of her need for him, all of him, but she'd needed to be with him because she'd simply been unable to keep away. She'd wanted *his* hug. Wanted his arms around her. She missed him.

'Sunday morning sex. The best ever.' He stroked her shoulder, his tone soft. 'Lucy didn't mind you coming out?'

'I didn't ask. It was the middle of the night, Lewis. They were both fine and well and fast asleep, and I'm not planning on staying long. No harm done. They won't even know I'm gone.'

'Oh. You're not staying?'

Feeling his frown against her neck, she turned round to look at him. 'Don't frown, Lewis. You know I have to go. It's just like old times, right? I have to be back in my bed before everyone wakes up. We have maybe another hour.'

'Makes it even more foolish to waste more time, then.' He pushed her hair back from her face and kissed her again. This time it was slow and tender and filled with so much emotion, it made her heart ache.

How could they be just friends when there was this much emotion between them, this much connection? Was it too early to talk about what next? Yes, it was too early. She couldn't push him into a corner. Better to enjoy this silly, fun sex.

She broke the kiss and snuggled into the crook of his arm, closing her eyes, her head on his chest. He wrapped his other arm round her and she felt the strong, steady beat of his heart against her ribcage.

None of this felt silly. It felt consequential. Her heart had opened to him again. She stroked his forearm and closed her eyes. Being held like this made her feel as if nothing in the world could hurt her. She felt safe and secure. Nothing bad could happen in this haven of his strength, of their… their what? Their craving? Their need? Their love?

Love?

What?

Her eyes flickered open. Had she fallen in love with him again?

Had she ever stopped loving him?

Had she? She'd tried. She'd moved to the other side of the world to stop loving him but it hadn't worked. So the simple answer was no. And the

most difficult, heart-wrenching answer was still…
no. She'd always loved him and, instead of dimming, it was growing, glowing brighter and stronger. And she couldn't help it, she couldn't stop it.

And so what if…what if he didn't feel the same?
What if…? She knew the 'what if?' Her stomach went into freefall.

Stupid, stupid, stupid Charlie.

He wanted kids and she couldn't have them—end of. That was the brutal truth. He would tell her it didn't matter. And she'd have to watch him coo at other people's babies and keep on pretending.

And her heart would break.

Oblivious to the sudden crisis in her heart, he lazily drew circles over her hip as he said, 'One thing I regret…well, I regret a lot of things about how we broke up…but we should have talked more…'

He didn't finish the sentence.

Completely alert now, she propped herself up on her elbow to look at him. 'What do you mean?'

His eyes were closed, but his breathing hitched. 'I was too closed off. But…' His voice trailed off again, as if he was rethinking the sentence or the whole conversation.

'But *what*, Lewis?'

He looked at her, eyes dark, haunted almost. Then he shook his head, as if shaking away his thoughts. 'It's… Ah, look, nothing. It's…too heavy for this time of night. You have to go soon, and that's okay.' He smiled but it was kind of sad. 'You have other commitments now.'

But…what?

Should we adopt? What about surrogacy? How about fostering? How about moving back in to-gether? How about my giving up all my hopes and dreams for you? How about falling deeper in love? Were those the things he meant, those things he wasn't actually going to say again? The things he didn't want to talk about.

All the emotions were tangling up inside her and the only respite she ever seemed to have was when they were making love. For a few amaz-ing minutes she could forget the past, but then it would barrel into her, along with all the reasons why they couldn't do this. 'Please, Lewis, I want to hear what you have to say.'

He rolled onto his back and stared up at the ceiling.

She waited, barely breathing.

He looked at her briefly, then away. 'We can't have kids.'

'*I* can't have kids, Lewis. You? You could prob-ably have a whole football team of mini-mes if you wanted to.'

His eyes flashed at her words and that hurt her the most. He had options. He had a chance and he still wanted that; he could not refute the ob-vious minute flicker of hope at her words. But he shook his head. 'There are other ways to be happy, right?'

'Like what? Please don't say you'll give up your dream for me. Please don't give up your chance for a family, to be a dad. And please don't put that decision on me.'

He frowned. 'What do you mean?'

Okay, so they were going to talk about this. It felt as if a huge weight was crushing her chest. 'I don't want you to promise me something and then regret it down the line. Give me up for a woman who can give you children. I couldn't bear that.'

'Charlie. Please don't think like that. That's not what I'm saying. I'm saying you must never give up that hope.'

'Oh, the hope thing again?' She sighed, her heart hurting. They'd been down this road before. *Keep believing, Charlie. Everything's going to be okay.* Things had not been okay.

His jaw tightened. 'There are other things we could do.'

'Like get a dog?'

'Yes, if you want. But there's also adoption or surrogacy.'

Oh. Okay.

Breathing out, she ventured, 'In New Zealand? The odds are very much against us. There aren't enough babies up for adoption and surrogacy has to be altruistic; it's not like we can pay someone to have a baby for us.'

But there was a chance. It wasn't impossible. A tiny flicker of hope fluttered in her chest. They were talking about this. *We*: he was talking about them as a couple. He was considering options.

Which meant things had gone too far already. Because no amount of wanting him to say that he loved her, that nothing could come between them or that they had options, would change the facts. The same facts that had influenced their breakup. He still wanted a child of his own, regardless of what he said. She could see the longing every time he looked at a child or held a baby. And she couldn't give him one.

More than that…so much more…she wouldn't be able to bear seeing his realisation that he'd chosen the wrong woman. She couldn't risk him leaving her. That was something she'd never recover from. She was scared of the strength of her feelings for him and the vulnerability that instilled in her.

Because she loved him. She'd never stopped loving him. Hell, she'd adored him since sixth form and that love still burned strong inside her. But it was one thing to love him from a distance, another to love him up close…and wait for the truth to dawn on him that she would not be enough.

Her phone from downstairs intruded into the weighted silence. She held her breath and listened. 'Did you hear that?'

'Your phone?' He sat up.

'It's the early hours; everyone should be asleep. It's either Lucy or our parents.' Neither of them phoning at this time would be good news. 'I've got to go see who it is. It could be important.'

Throwing on his T-shirt, she ran down to the lounge, grabbed her phone from her bag and her heart constricted.

'It's Lucy,' she shouted up to Lewis. 'There must be something wrong. She never rings me.' She pressed the answer buttons and heard her sister's terrified cries. 'Charlie, please, where are you? I need you. Please come home. Please.'

'Wh-what's happened?' Charlie could only imagine something terrible.

A sob came, then another. 'Please just come home.'

'Of course. I'm on my way.' Her heart drummed against her ribcage as she turned to Lewis who was now standing in front of her, dressed in T-shirt and shorts. 'I've got to go.'

Face set in determination, he nodded. 'I'll grab your clothes. I'm coming with you.'

But she put her hand on his chest, shaking her head.

This was all her fault. She'd sneaked out instead of staying where she would have been all along. She'd given in to temptation, put her own needs first again. Her needs before those of Lewis...who would have been asleep still if she hadn't come booty calling. Her needs before those of her her sister and her niece.

Lewis's dark eyes bored into her. She knew him well enough to know he wanted to help and didn't like not being able to. Feeling helpless was something she'd experienced for a while; she knew exactly how it felt.

'No. No, Lewis. You can't come with me. I'm sorry.' She needed to be with her sister. Just the two of them, not with Lewis.

Not Lewis. Stark reality hit her hard: not Lewis…

They couldn't keep doing this and pretending everything would work out well. She couldn't keep bruising her heart. She had to, finally, put a stop to this. She shook her head again, not wanting to say things she knew she had to say. She'd said them all once before then she'd walked away.

He looked at her and a dozen questions ran across his gaze. She shook her head.

Don't make me say anything else. They'd got carried away.

But he squeezed her hand; either he didn't realise what she was trying to say or he didn't want to acknowledge it. 'Okay, you know where I am if you need me.'

'Thanks. But this is something I need to do on my own.'

Words she'd said before. She walked to the door and closed it behind her, heart aching, all on repeat.

It wasn't any easier the second time around.

* * *

She found Lucy bent over the toilet bowl, her eyes red-rimmed, her pale, too-thin body shaking inside her winter pyjamas. Fleecy pyjamas in the height of summer—poor Lucy was always cold these days. Charlie gasped, ran across the cold tiles and wrapped her arms round her sister's shoulders. 'Hey, girl. Lucy, what's wrong, darling?'

Her sister groaned. 'I've been attached to this loo for the last hour and I feel like absolute crap. But...' She held up a fistful of her beautiful Titian hair and her face crumpled. 'Worse than anything else, my hair's falling out, in clumps.'

The Rose crowning glory, the hair they'd hated and loved in equal measure growing up. They'd been warned it would happen after the chemo but it wasn't something they'd really talked about, maybe hoping they'd never have to face it. Charlie felt tears pricking her eyes but she forced them back. She would be her sister's tower of strength here. She would not cry. 'Oh, honey, I'm so sorry.'

Lucy sat back looking defeated and dejected. 'I wasn't ready for this to happen. I pretended I was going to be different to everyone else. I know I shouldn't care about how I look, but I do. I don't want to be bald. I don't want...any of this.'

Charlie's heart felt as if it were breaking from leaving Lewis amidst such confusion, and now seeing her sister in pieces. 'It's cruel, Lucy.'

'Yes, it is. I don't want this. I just want to be able to spend happy, lovely time with my daughter and my sister. Bloody cancer. And I'm ranting now too.' She gave a sniff and the faintest hint of a rueful smile. 'Sorry about that too.'

'You can rant and shout and scream all you need. None of this is fair, none of it. Not the lump or the cancer or the surgery or the chemo that makes you sick. And definitely not your beautiful hair. But if your hair's falling out, it means the medicine is working, right?'

'I suppose.' Lucy wiped her eyes with the back of her hand. 'I'm sorry if I gave you a fright. Were you at Lewis's house?'

Oh, Lewis... They hadn't finished their conversation and everything was up in the air. Neither of them had been brave enough to face the truth and say it. They'd grasped at one more chance to be together, to sink into each other's arms. 'Yes. I was only gone a couple of hours. I was about to head home anyway.'

'I'm sorry I interrupted your night.'

Charlie squeezed her sister in a warm hug. 'Never say sorry for what you're going through, Luce. I love you. *I'm* sorry I wasn't here when you needed me.'

'You are, hun. You're here all of the time. You work, sleep and look after me. I know that.'

She wiped her sister's forehead with a damp

flannel then helped her to stand. 'I won't leave you again, I promise.'

But Lucy chuckled and put her head on Charlie's shoulder, leaning heavily on her as they walked slowly to her bedroom. 'Hey, don't make promises you can't keep.'

Charlie had tried to tell Lewis that, hadn't she? That good intentions were just that: good intentions. They weren't fixed in stone. Not that she'd ever leave her sister again to cope with this on her own, but she could. Just like Lewis could promise to stay with her and then leave when someone or something else came along. That was the risk, wasn't it, the risk with love? You put all your dreams into one person and hoped they'd stick with you. Hoped they'd stay.

Lucy slumped heavily on to her bed. Charlie lifted her sister's legs under the sheets and surreptitiously disposed of the fallen copper strands on her pillow. Her mind was made up. 'Well, obviously I'll be at work some of the time, but I'll be here for you, Lucy. Always. Lewis… Well, Lewis is only going to be a friend from now on. A proper friend, nothing more.'

'Don't put yourself second. Live your life, Charlie. You have so much to give.'

Not the right things for Lewis, though.

'I'm here. I'm not going anywhere.'

But he'd broached the subject of options, something they'd never managed to do five years ago. He'd brought it up. He'd been thinking about it.

I'm not going anywhere.

Why did she believe herself and not Lewis?

Because she knew that vows and promises could be broken by hardship and struggle. She knew, because she'd broken them herself.

So how could she trust anyone else to stay when she hadn't?

CHAPTER SIXTEEN

HE'D HANDLED IT BADLY. He'd clammed up right at the time when he should have been more open. But he hadn't known where they stood, especially after agreeing it had just been a friend thing, a booty call. Had it just been fun or was it more? Now it couldn't be anything, he realised that, because she'd be terrified of leaving her sister again.

He knocked on the front door, wondering whether this was a mistake. Charlie opened the door and peered out with wary, tired eyes. She was wearing cute shortie pyjamas, her hair was messy and, given that it was four o'clock in the afternoon, that was unusual. But she gave him a small smile. 'Hey. This is a surprise.'

'You left your purse. Thought I'd drop it by in case you needed it.' He held it out to her.

She opened the door a little further and took her purse from him. 'Thanks. It must have fallen out of my bag when I was in such a hurry to get back here.'

'Not surprising. You left in a whirl of panic. I thought I might see you at work to give it back to you, but they tell me you've been off for a few days.'

'Yes. I've taken a couple of carer's days.'

He should have known that, if they'd been involved in any way. But she hadn't answered his messages and hadn't sent any of her own. What was he meant to do with that—just walk away? Pretend that they hadn't made love or that they hadn't reconnected deeper and harder than before? 'I wanted to make sure you're okay. I don't want to come in, I just wanted to let you know I'm here for you. How's Lucy?'

Charlie's voice softened and she smiled sadly. 'She's trying to get some sleep. The chemo makes her sick and now her hair's falling out too.'

He looked at Charlie's messy beautiful hair and his gut lurched. 'Damn. I'm so sorry. You know there are charities that can help her feel better about the way she looks?'

'Yeah. I grabbed some leaflets from work last week. I just haven't got round to reading any of them yet.'

He watched as guilt flitted across her face. 'It's not a sin to want some relief for yourself too.'

'You mean sneaking out in the middle of the night?' Her eyebrows rose. 'Like a teenager?'

'Yeah. Time out.'

'Well, I'm not a teenager, Lewis. And nothing you can say will make me feel better about not being here when my sister needed me.' She shook her head and he knew that that conversation was dead in the water before it began.

A little cry came from inside the house.

'Ugh. Stella needs entertaining and we're both exhausted. Bless her.' She looked distraught, torn, sad and guilty all rolled into one. She turned round and called out, 'Hush, sweetie. It's okay, Stella baby, I'm coming.'

Here was something he could help with, at least. 'Do you want me to take her out for an hour, so you can get some rest?'

'Oh.' She blinked and looked sorely tempted but shook her head, raising her voice over the increasingly loud cries. 'Oh, well…no. No, thanks all the same.'

'You could do with some rest too, right? The carers need to be cared for.'

She pressed her lips together. The connection they'd had on Sunday morning was hanging by a thread. He could see she'd closed herself off. She was barely coping with her responsibilities here. Did she feel he was a responsibility too?

Finally, she nodded. 'Okay, yes. Thanks, Lewis. I owe you.'

'You owe me nothing. It's okay, I've got plenty of time. I'm on earlies this week.' Although he'd have moved heaven and earth to help her, taken carer's days off too if she'd needed him to, phoned in sick or given up his damned job. Because, regardless of what she told him, or how much he tried to convince himself otherwise, he was hard-wired to be her champion, her cheerleader and her supporter.

She opened the door wide and let him in. Stella was sitting in the play pen in the lounge, bawling her eyes out, so he picked her up and soothed her, rocking her against his chest. 'Hey, hey. Look at you, clever girl. You were sitting up all by yourself. What's the matter? Was no one here? Auntie Charlie was just talking to me. So much noise from one so little! What is it? There's no need to cry.'

As if by some miracle the little girl stopped crying and stared at him. She patted his cheek with her hand as she inhaled shuddering breaths, then she smiled.

He grinned back. 'That's better. Now, should we go for a walk, see what we can find at the park? Shall we go? Oh, butter wouldn't melt now, right?'

From behind him he heard a sharp intake of breath; or was it a strained, throaty cry…?

He turned to see Charlie striding towards him, arms outstretched for the baby. 'Actually, it's time for her nap. I'll take her for a quick walk round the block later.'

'I can do that. You look bushed.'

'No, Lewis.' Her tone was sharp enough to make him stop in his tracks.

Okay. She's tired and stressed.

He kissed Stella on the cheek and put her back

into the playpen. Then he walked towards Charlie, his gut tightening in a knot. Her mouth was set in a line and he knew, just knew, that her tone wasn't just because she was tired and stressed; it was far more than that. He knew, soul-deep, this was the end.

Not again. Don't do this again.

He shook his head, not wanting her to say the words, not wanting to hear them. 'Before you say anything final, hear me out. I can wait… I will wait for you, Charlie. I'll wait as long as I have to until you're freed up a little.'

She walked to the front door, then outside, and he couldn't do anything but follow. She stopped on the path and turned to him. 'No, Lewis. You cannot wait for me. I don't know how long this will take. Lucy needs me and I need to take care of her. This isn't something you can fix for me.'

But I want to.

'No, I get that. But I can be here for you. I can help, or just be at the end of the phone.'

They'd never finished their important conversation.

She shook her head, resolute. 'I don't think that's a good idea. I'm not sure we can even stay friends, not the way things are between us.'

'You mean the way we're good together? The way we make each other feel? The way we keep coming back to each other even after everything that happened? We're divorced, Charlie. We've lived apart for five years and missed so much of each other's lives and yet none of that matters, none of it, because I believe in us.'

Her hand flew to her mouth. 'Please. Don't.'

'So you're going to walk way *again*?' His heart felt cleaved in two.

It wasn't supposed to have got this intense. He hadn't wanted to feel this much. He was meant to have protected himself from this very scenario. And yet here he was, trying to make her see sense again. Because he knew that they could have something very special, could be happy together, if they gave it a shot. If she did.

She swallowed, looking as hurt as he felt. 'Last time I had to go for *me*. I needed space to lick my wounds and come to terms with my infertility. This time it's for you.'

'For me? That's bull, Charlie.' He knew his tone was becoming sharp too and he tried to soften it. 'You haven't even asked what I want.'

'Because I already know. We were just about to talk about it, the other morning, right? Really talk about what we might do as a…couple. How you're willing to put your wants and needs second to mine. But we don't know if we can adopt, or find a surrogate. We don't know if we'd be lucky enough to be chosen to be parents. That's a very uncertain future for someone who's desperate to be a daddy.

'I don't want to wake up one morning and see

regret in your eyes, Lewis. Regret that you made the wrong choice, and a realisation that you could have what you want with someone else. So we can't be a couple, Lewis. I won't let it happen. I won't let either of us take that risk. I don't want to have my heart broken again and I imagine you don't want that either.'

It was already breaking; couldn't she see that? She was breaking him, breaking this amazing thing they could have together. 'We don't walk away when things get tough, Charlie. We stay. We stay and we fight. I would never walk away.'

'I know. I know you'd try to stay to the bitter end. You'd fight and fight and fight.' She put her palm up. 'So please don't make this harder than it has to be. We both knew coming into it that there were huge barriers. Nothing can change facts, Lewis. I am not the right person for you.

'I'm okay with what life has thrown at me. I know I can be fulfilled and happy without having kids. I've come to terms with a child-free future. I am a fantastic auntie and godmother and a great doctor. I have so many amazing plans for travel, and for my life. I am whole and I am thriving. But, every time I see you with Stella, I see that longing ripple through you. I can't trust that you won't decide to leave me. And I couldn't live every day waiting for it to happen.'

'You don't believe it when I tell you I'll wait? That I'll stay? I'll be here for you, Charlie, always. But, hell you can't *trust* me?' That was the lowest blow. Even after everything he'd said and done, she didn't think he had staying power. 'You walked away last time, Charlie, not me.'

He knew he should be walking away now, relieved that she'd set him free. But his feet were lead, his limbs too heavy to move. He didn't feel free, he felt broken.

She put her hand on his arm. 'I know, more than anyone, how sometimes you have to escape for your own sanity. And I couldn't bear to see you do the same. I'm sorry, Lewis.'

'So am I.' He shook his arm and got her to take her hand away. If she touched him again, he'd fold. 'But I'm not sure how you can say you want to leave when you were talking about love only the other day.'

She blinked, shock flashing across her expression. 'When?'

'In the car park. When we were making out.' His heart had swollen in panic but also comfort and relief.

Her eyes widened as the memory hit her. 'Oh, Lewis. I said "I love the way you kiss me". I love your smile, yes. I love lots of things about you—'

'But you don't love me enough to stay.'

She looked up at him, her eyes swimming with tears. Her mouth trembled and he could see she was trying hard not to cry. 'No, Lewis. That's the problem, don't you see? I love you too much to stay.'

Then she walked up the path and closed the door.

She was gone—again.

He stared at the red paint.

She did love him.

He rubbed his forehead with the heel of his hand then stalked up to the door to hammer on it. To tell her to come back out and that they'd sort it all. Make her believe that he'd stay. Make her understand.

But Lucy... Stella... He couldn't disturb them and add to her problems.

He heard the baby start to cry again and heard someone cooing in a cracked voice, then an adult sob.

Charlie. Come back.

He walked down the path then back up again.

How the hell could he convince her that this time they could work it through?

He kicked the doorstep and slumped down on it.

'Charlie,' he whispered. 'For God's sake.'

How would he survive seeing her every day at work? How would she survive seeing him? How would he cope hearing her voice, her laughter? How would he be able to hand over a patient when there was this chasm between them?

He put his head in his hands.

Oh, Charlie, why the hell are you doing this to us?

How would he ever get over her second time round?

'Who was at the door?' Lucy croaked as she sat down at the kitchen table. 'Did I hear someone?'

'It was Lewis.' Charlie put a bowl of home-made chicken soup in front of her sister, then sat down in front of her own food, but she had no appetite.

Lucy frowned. 'He didn't want to come in?'

'Oh, he did.' Charlie tried to control herself. She'd been stuffing back the tears the whole time she'd been playing with Stella, putting on that false happy voice as she'd read to her from the little cloth book, trying to get her to go to sleep. She'd pretended she was okay when she'd chopped the carrots and onions. She'd forced herself to hold back when she'd called Lucy down for dinner. 'I ended it.'

'What?' Lucy's sunken eyes fizzed with shock as she reached over the table for Charlie's hand. 'Why?'

Charlie put up her palm. 'Don't. Please don't. If you touch me or say one single nice thing, I'll cry.'

Lucy scraped her chair back, went over and wrapped her arms around Charlie. 'Cry all you want, sis. I'm here.'

But Charlie squeezed her eyelids closed, pressing back the threatening tears. 'I'm okay. It's for the best. It is.'

She had to keep telling herself that. She had to believe it. She needed to forget him.

Her gaze fell on the leaflets scattered on the console. Leaflets about a charity that ran programmes to support women going through chemotherapy and hair loss. About another one that did free counselling, one that provided wigs, another that accepted hair donations and another that raised money for cancer charities by running head shaves. There was help for everything Lucy was going through and more. Charlie determined to put all her focus on her sister to help her reach out for this available support.

Maybe then she might forget Lewis.

Fat chance, when she'd see him most days.

Maybe then things wouldn't hurt so much.

Fat chance, because real, honest, true love didn't fade, did it? She knew that already. She'd been there, trying to forget her marriage and Lewis for five years, and had learnt that she would not, could not, forget him. She loved him more now than ever before.

She cleared her throat and picked up the leaflets, unable to meet her sister's piercing and enquiring gaze. 'Hey, why don't we take a look through these? Maybe we can contact a couple of these places tomorrow?'

'Charlie, look at me. *Look at me.* Stop deflecting.' Lucy stepped back and peered at her. 'Oh, honey. You are so not okay.'

Charlie's throat felt raw and thick. She couldn't pretend to her sister that she was all right when she was actually falling to pieces. She was trying not to say the words again, because they were barbs in her heart, but they were stuck in her gullet and she couldn't say or swallow anything unless she set them free. 'I love him, Lucy.'

Lucy stroked Charlie's hair. 'I know you do. So I don't understand why you ended it. And, God, please don't say you did it because you're looking after me.'

'No. Not for you, for me. I wish we'd never started up again.' She shook her head. 'No. That's not true. It's been lovely, really lovely. I just wish it didn't all hurt this much.' It was twice as bad as last time because he'd changed, and so had she. They'd become wiser, bolder and more willing to share their feelings. He'd changed so much for the better.

Truth was, there was no better man than Lewis Parry. And she'd lost him again. The hurt and sadness swelled through her until it threatened to overpower her. She stood up on wobbly legs. 'Sorry. I'll be back in a minute.'

She flung back her chair, not wanting her sister to see her in such a state. Then she ran up to her room and flopped on her bed.

And finally gave in to the tears and grief.

CHAPTER SEVENTEEN

'COME ON, MATE, it's for charity.' Brin steered the van into the beach-side car park and pulled on the hand brake. 'The team are relying on you.'

Lewis shrugged, the lethargy that had been dogging him for the last two weeks feeling worse, not better. He stared at the ocean, choppy and churning today, kind of how he felt too: roiling, swirling, out of sorts. 'I don't feel like going out.'

'Which means you need to.' Brin nudged him, about to take a bite out of his chicken and cranberry pie. 'You can't keep moping around like this. To be brutally honest, you're becoming a bit of a tragic.'

'I'm not moping. Or tragic.' Lewis shook his head and stared at the soggy sandwich he'd brought with him for lunch. He missed her. He hated seeing her at work and feeling the awkwardness between them. Hated the short, patient-focused conversations, the sadness in her eyes, the pain. Hated hearing her laughter and not being part of the joke or the fun. 'I don't feel like being sociable.'

Brin turned to him. 'Well, you have to. You're

Mr Charity. You run up buildings…you bid too much in auctions… You have to come with us.'

'I don't, actually.'

'No, mate. You don't have to do anything. You can just never go out again. Sit around all day like a bear with a sore head. Actually, I'd prefer it if you did actually snap or growl. I'm not a huge fan of this sullen apathy.' Brin took a mouthful of pie and they sat in a loaded silence.

Lewis put his uneaten sandwich back in the container. 'I'm not apathetic. I come to work, do my job.'

'Then go home again and do nothing. You know, I haven't heard you talking about your running or training recently. You haven't been to any of the team nights out. You just…exist.' Brin's expression softened. 'I'm worried about you.'

'No need.' But Brin was right. Ever since Charlie had closed that doo, Lewis had lost his sense of fun and humour. Not wanting to ruin the vibe, he'd skipped Lily's ballet concert and had got a rap from his brother for his absence.

Bad Uncle Lewis.

Bad colleague Lewis.

Bad friend Lewis.

Yeah, okay, so maybe he was feeling sorry for himself.

Brin fixed him with his gaze. 'You know you're going to have to try to forget her…or win her back.'

'Who?' He hadn't discussed Charlie with Brin, apart from telling him to back off with his match-making.

Brin chortled. 'You know who.'

'I can't win her back if she doesn't want me.'

'I saw the way she looked at you, mate. I heard…' Brin shook his head and winced. 'Oh, never mind.'

'Heard what?' Lewis's gut tightened.

'I heard you talking in Harper's room. The baby monitor was on.' Brin screwed up his face. 'Sorry.'

'What exactly did you hear?' Lewis cringed. They'd thought the monitor was off. They hadn't seen a light on it.

'Something about wanting more… Struggling to keep away from you…' Brin's face bloomed red. 'As soon as I realised you were in there I turned the app off, honest.'

Lewis swore. 'Oh, God. Embarrassing.'

'Or witness to how much you care about each other.'

'Well, forget whatever you heard. She's broken it off. We're done.'

'And you're just going to take it? Not fight?' Brin frowned. 'Surely if you got back together so quickly there's something worth fighting for? Remember what I did when I fell love with Mia and decided to fight for her, for us?'

'Gave me notice on your job. Yeah, I remember.

And also asked for the job back when you both admitted your feelings for each other.'

Charlie had told him she loved him. He hadn't done that. He hadn't told her the depth of his feelings. Maybe he should have. 'I don't think admitting anything is going to help.'

But there was a kernel of something bright and hopeful in his chest. She wanted him to open up, didn't she?

'Well, anything's worth a try, right?'

'I don't know.' Lewis checked the time. 'We need to head off.'

'Okay.' His colleague sighed heavily and handed him a leaflet that had been stuffed in the glove compartment with other detritus. 'Look, I don't want to sound like I'm nagging, but this is the biggest charity event of the season. Some of our team are having their heads shaved to support the cancer patients. It's the biggest money-raiser they have all year. You've got to come support us.'

'You're going to get your head shaved?' How had he missed that? But then, he'd not been focusing on anything except getting through work so he could go home and…okay…mope a bit.

'Yes, I told you.' Brin tutted and shook his head. 'Me and Emma and Raj.'

Lucy. Charlie had been distraught about Lucy losing her hair.

Charlie. He couldn't help them in person but

he could do this—give money to the people that helped them.

For the first time in the last couple of weeks he felt the fog in his brain start to shift. He had a purpose. 'Okay.'

She did care for him. She loved him. And where there was love there was hope.

He'd go to the event then he'd go round and see her, try to get her to understand things from his point of view.

He'd let her go last time. This time he was going to fight a damned sight harder.

Charlie watched from the side of the stage as the compere announced the final event of the fund-raising evening. She'd kept a low profile backstage, because she hadn't felt like talking to anyone, but she kind of wished she'd had a couple of drinks, because what she was about to do scared her to death. But if Lucy was going through it then the least Charlie could do was show her support by doing it too.

She took a deep breath and headed to the back of the small queue of people waiting to go on stage.

'Charlie?'

She turned to the sound of a male voice, her heart jumping, then diving. 'Brin! Hi. Are you going for the big shave too?'

Brin was standing in front of her with a couple of other paramedics she recognised from work.

He ran his fingers over his short hair. 'Not that it'll make much difference to my head, but I've got quite a few sponsors, so hopefully it'll raise a bit of cash.'

'Good on you.' She tugged her hair out of the ponytail and ran her fingers through the strands, easing out any knots. It would make a massive difference to her, and the money she was going to raise would help the charity.

The compere called for the first three people to come up to the stage. She stood with Brin and watched them go. She heard the chatter and the audience clapping, the buzz of the razor.

Her heart quickened. Her stomach lurched. Was this a good idea? What would Lucy say? Or Lewis, when he saw her at work?

Oh, Lewis. She missed him so much.

The next three went. She closed her eyes and tried to steady her nerves.

There was more talking, and cheering this time. There was snipping and buzzing. Everyone's motivation and story was similar to hers. People were shaving their heads for loved ones who were going through treatments, in memory of people who had passed or for those who had got through and were living their full lives. People just wanting to help somehow.

'Good luck,' Brin called to her as he stepped on to the stage.

'You too.'

I'm going to need it. I also need a hug.

A Lewis hug in particular. She knew without a doubt that he'd hate her shaving off her hair, but would also support her one hundred percent. Because he was her supporter, her cheerleader. Always had been.

There wasn't a single minute of her day when she didn't miss him. For five long years she'd learnt to get along without him, but now—after only a few weeks back in his presence, in his arms and in his bed—she could not get him out of her mind. It was as if her body couldn't function without him but needed him to fully live, to breathe.

But it was for the best.

It was—for his best, not hers.

Then it was her turn. She stepped on to the stage, her legs shaking just a little. *Be brave.* This was only a shave; she wasn't going to endure anything like Lucy was.

She'd devoted every spare minute to looking after her sister and niece. Last week they'd got word that Lucy was responding better than expected to the treatment. There were still long days ahead but the news had given them all a lift. For the first time since she'd closed the door on any kind of relationship with Lewis, she'd felt positive.

But hell, she'd ached to call him and tell him the good news. To share their milestones with him. To share her life.

She sat down and looked out at the crowd. There

must have been five hundred people in the auditorium but in the sea of faces only one stood out.

Lewis.

Her heart hammered. Lewis was here; of course he was. He was supporting his colleagues, as he always did. He was that kind of guy—good, kind and compassionate.

He was sexy, fun, gorgeous and lovable. So loved...

The microphone was thrust into her hands and she was asked about her motivation for doing this. She cleared her throat and her eyes locked with his. He hadn't known she'd be here, that was obvious. She shifted her gaze away from his shocked one to somewhere in the middle of the crowd, because she couldn't look at him without crying.

'I'm doing this to raise money for cancer care. My sister's going through a hard time with chemotherapy at the moment and I wanted to show her she wasn't on her own. To show her that she is loved and that no one going through cancer treatment need be alone. Believe that you are loved and that we will walk this journey with you. Whatever it takes, we'll stay by your side.'

We'll stay.

She hadn't. She'd left him when things had got tough, and had chosen to walk away instead of staying and fighting. Because she was scared of being left on her own—something she'd never been allowed to do—she'd made it happen. She'd got in there first. She'd chosen that path because staying and hoping *he* wouldn't leave her had been worse. She hadn't been able to bear watching him realise he'd made the wrong choice. Hadn't been able to bear seeing the disappointment on her parents' faces or on Lewis's.

There came a round of applause, then the hairdresser walked forward.

Heart thumping, Charlie looked over at the place where Lewis had been sitting, but he wasn't there. Had he walked out? He'd always loved her hair. Was he angry that she was shaving her hair off? Her throat filled with the swell of tears. She felt sure he'd somehow have managed to convince her not to do this.

Oh, Lewis.

'I want to donate my hair for wigs, please. It's not dyed and in good condition.'

'Great. It's lovely and long. I'll tie it back, because it's easier to cut off all in one go.' The hairdresser nodded and gathered Charlie's hair into ponytail. 'Are you ready?'

Was she? She took a deep breath, sad to her core that Lewis hadn't been able to sit and watch. 'Sure am.'

She listened to the *snip-snip* of the scissors close to her head, then the hairdresser held up her cut ponytail to the cheers and applause of the crowd. Then all she could hear was the thud-thud of her heart in her ears. Then the buzzing, first up the back.

'It's a bit cold.' She laughed nervously.

The hairdresser didn't answer. The crowd gasped.

'Do I look that bad?' Charlie asked.

'No. You look beautiful. You're always beautiful to me, Charlie.'

That voice. That tone. That man. *Lewis.*

She closed her eyes as she felt his fingers run over the tufts of hair she had left. Lewis was shaving her head. Her hands curled into fists as she tried to stop herself from crying. 'No. You can't do this. Stop. You love my hair.'

'I love you, Charlie Jade Rose. I love *you.* Your hair is icing.' He came to stand in front of her, crouched and looked her in the eyes. 'I'm not going anywhere. If you want to do this, then I want to help and support you. I love you. And if you love someone, you stay. You stay for the good and the bad. You stay.'

'You love me?'

No. No. No. No. That would make everything ten times worse.

'Of course, Charlie. I've never stopped. If it's possible, I love you more now than ever.'

'Then you have to leave now. Go. Please.' She grabbed his arm. 'Please. Don't make this any worse for me.'

'I'm not going anywhere.' He flicked the razor on and shaved one side, then the next. Then he took the microphone from the compere and said, 'Charlotte Rose, you are incredible. You have donated your lovely hair to be made into a wig so someone else can feel more like themselves when they're going through challenging times. And then you've allowed me to shave your hair completely off. You look…' he inhaled and shook his head, staring at her as if she was a model '…truly the most beautiful I have ever seen you.'

The audience gasped as one.

'How much have you raised?' he asked her.

He loves me. He thinks I'm beautiful. He's told me in front of all these people.

She couldn't believe what she was hearing. 'Um…for the charity? I think about fifteen hundred.'

'Brilliant.' He nodded. 'If you shave my hair, I'll double it.'

The crowd erupted in cheers, stamping their feet and clapping. The compere handed round orange buckets for donations and there was nothing she could do but change places.

She held the razor and took a breath. Because she couldn't allow herself to get all carried away like the audience. There were still insurmountable obstacles here. 'I love you, Lewis. I love you so much and I miss you. But there is no future for us. I've seen you with Stella. You need to be a dad.'

Not wanting to hear his answer, she set about shaving his head, starting at the back then the sides and then the top. In a few minutes she was done. And, hell, he looked beautiful too.

Just as she thought he'd given up on an answer, he took her razor-free hand. 'I love you, Charlie. Any way you are. With or without hair. With or without a baby, or a family. Nothing else matters. I love everything about you. I will always love you as you are, wholly, fully.'

She looked at the floor, at his hair mingling with hers and the drops of her tears. 'But…'

He put the microphone down and spoke directly to her. 'Listen to me, Charlie. You always told me I should put my needs first. Well, here I am, knowing what I need, standing up for what I need, telling you what I need.

'It's *you*, Charlie. *I need you.* If you want to explore surrogacy or adoption or any other options, then we can do exactly that. Whatever you want— whatever *we* want. We can talk about it; we can investigate it together. Because we do have options, being a parent isn't about blood ties, I know that from experience. And if children don't happen, then that will be absolutely fine too. We have four little girls who want our love. We can be the most doting auntie and uncle in the world. I have everything I need right here with you. I promise that *you* are all I need, Charlie. You *are* my family.'

She thought about Lucy, Stella and their little family of two. That was enough for her sister.

She thought about how she'd stayed with Lucy,

not out of obligation but out of pure love. 'Don't put yourself second,' she'd told him and he'd promised her that nothing else mattered because he loved her so much. The same way she'd promised those things to Lucy because she loved her. She'd do anything for her, willingly and happily.

Was that how he felt—that selfless love for someone else, for *her*? No expectations, no conditions, just love.

She saw him now, doing this—shaving her head, having his head shaved. An act of true love, love that was inspiring and deep. He'd told her he loved her since high school and she'd loved him right back, even when she'd tried hard not to. That love had coddled her, fuelled her and now filled her with absolute joy. Their love was enduring and ever-lasting.

And, finally, she allowed herself to believe him. He would stay. Whatever happened, he would stay. And so would she. 'Oh, Lewis. I love you so, so much.'

But he bent down on one knee. 'So, Charlie Jade Rose…'

'Oh! What are you doing?' She blinked at him and then at the audience.

The crowd whistled and cheered. She heard the *thunk-thunk-thunk* of coins being thrown into the buckets. Whatever else happened, they'd raised a lot more money for the charity than she'd hoped for. She smiled as she looked down at her beautiful man.

He took her hand. 'I thought, given that our wedding was the best ever, we might have a rerun. What do you think? Will you marry me, Charlie Rose, all over again?'

'Oh, yes. Of course. Yes!' She pulled him up and he took her into his arms—exactly where she was meant to be.

The crowd went wild.

One year later...

'Trying to co-ordinate four little bridesmaids and an eighteen-month-old flower girl is like herding cats.' Lucy grinned as she picked up Stella and smacked a kiss on her chubby cheek. 'Now, go with Lily. Let her help you throw the petals on to the path while Mummy walks in front of Auntie Charlie.'

'You are the best flower girl I could ask for.' Charlie kissed Stella goodbye and watched Lily take the toddler to their places in preparation for the wedding procession. Then she gave her sister a hug, her beautiful, happy and very healthy sister. 'Thank you.'

'No, thank you for asking her to be flower girl. She doesn't quite understand but she loves twirling in her pretty dress.' Lucy grinned. 'I love what you've done with your hair.'

Charlie patted the cornflowers entwined in her

short pixie cut. 'Thanks. I'm going to keep it short, I think. It's a lot easier for work.'

'It suits you. And now we're all matchy-matchy.' She ran her fingertips over her short cut. The music began to play, the same tune they'd chosen for their first wedding. 'Now, where's Dad? Time to make your big entrance.'

Their parents had dashed back from Uganda two weeks after Charlie's head shave—and the moment Lucy had finally told them about her cancer—as both Lucy and Charlie had known they would. But they'd had their long-hoped-for overseas charity experience before moving in with Lucy and Stella and helping out. Somehow, they seemed to have mellowed a little, and only wanted to help, not domineer or take over.

And it had seemed an appropriate time then for a now homeless Charlie to move in with Lewis, and those empty seats at the dinner tables and social gatherings were filled again.

Their wedding was even better second time round. It was smaller, at the beach, with just family and a few close friends. Co-ordinating Lily, Lola, Luna, Harper and Stella all to stand still for the photos was the biggest and funniest challenge. Lewis wrapped his arms around Charlie's waist as they watched the girls skipping, jumping and wriggling and she leaned back against him.

'Five girls.' She laughed. 'Maybe one of our

siblings will have a boy some time. You must be getting over all the pink.'

'What? I've got my football team all sorted. Lily's my star attacker, Lola's in goals and Luna's showing great potential in midfield. Harper's more thoughtful and watchful, plus she's tall...probably good at centre back.' They watched as Stella waddled towards her mum then plopped down on the sand. 'Stella might need a little more training.'

'Aw. She's only been walking a few months.'

'Got to get them when they're young.' He laughed, then squeezed Charlie tightly and kissed her cheek. His love for his girls shone and made her heart sing with love—even more love, if that were possible.

They'd applied to the adoption agency and had advertised for surrogates but no luck so far. That didn't matter; if it happened, it happened. If not, then...they had each other, the four blood-tied nieces plus Harper who, they'd all decided, must become an honorary niece. Their lives were full of babysitting and school concerts, loud and chaotic lunches and laughter. They were one big family.

'Are you happy?' Lewis whispered against her throat.

He'd asked her that not long after they'd reconnected and she'd told him to ask her again when Lucy had finished her treatment. 'More than I thought I ever could be. I'm married to my best husband. I can say that because I've had two now.' She grinned up at him. 'My sister's improving every day. We have the most amazing friends and family.'

As if on cue, best-man-again Logan ambled over. 'Hey, I'm sorry, but the weather forecast isn't great for the evening. We'll have to bring the chairs and tables inside the venue. It's going to rain.'

They'd planned an early-evening dinner outside at a long table under the trees. But Lewis grinned as he turned to Charlie. 'You know what that means?'

She laughed. 'Flash flooding?'

'I damned well hope so.' His eyes twinkled as they both remembered their night in the fancy hotel.

'Me too. I love you, Lewis Parry.'

'I love you too, Charlie. Always have and always will.'

And now she believed him, with all her heart.

* * * * *

If you enjoyed this story, check out these other great reads from Louisa George

Reunited by the Nurse's Secret
Ivy's Fling with the Surgeon
Resisting the Single Dad Next Door
Cornish Reunion with the Heart Doctor

All available now!